'Almada combines reportage, fiction, and autobiography to explore femicide in Argentina in her acute, unflinching latest.'
Publishers Weekly (starred review)

'Part journalism, part history, part autobiography, part relentless nightmare.'
Shelf Awareness (starred review)

'Not an easy book, but an important one – a work of investigative writing about how easily women's lives are obscured.'
The Scotsman

'Almada's prose is sparse, but the details count. Her ear for dialogue and especially gossip is pitch perfect. Her eye for detail is hawkish.'
LA Review of Books

'A welcome new voice in Latin American storytelling.'
Kirkus

'Fate has in *Dead Girls* the perfume of a Greek tragedy: immutable, irreversible, lethal.'
El País

'An unassuming yet
The

First published by Charco Press 2020
Charco Press Ltd., Office 59, 44-46 Morningside Road, Edinburgh, EH10 4BF

Copyright © Selva Almada 2014
Published by arrangement with Agencia Literaria CBQ SL
First published in Spanish as *Chicas muertas* by
Random House Mondadori (Argentina)
English translation copyright © Annie McDermott 2020

The rights of Selva Almada to be identified as the author of this work and of Annie
McDermott to be identified as the translator of this work have been asserted by
them in accordance with the Copyright, Designs & Patents Act 1988.

Work published with funding from the 'Sur' Translation Support Programme
of the Ministry of Foreign Affairs of Argentina / Obra editada en el marco
del Programa 'Sur' de Apoyo a las Traducciones del Ministerio de Relaciones
Exteriores y Culto de la República Argentina.

A CIP catalogue record for this book is available from the British Library.

ISBN: 9781916277847
e-book: 9781916277854

www.charcopress.com

Edited by Fionn Petch
Cover designed by Pablo Font
Typeset by Laura Jones
Proofread by Fiona Mackintosh

4   6   8   10   9   7   5   3

Supported using public funding by
**ARTS COUNCIL
ENGLAND**

LOTTERY FUNDED

Selva Almada

DEAD GIRLS

Translated by
Annie McDermott

CHARCO PRESS

In memory of Andrea, María Luisa and Sarita

AUTHOR'S NOTE

I was born and raised in a provincial town, in what here we call 'the interior' of the country or *la Argentina profunda*. The 1980s, the decade of my small-town adolescence, were another world: no internet, no cable TV, barely any telephones (telephones had to be requested from the company, and it could be a decade or more before one was finally installed). In my house, for example, we didn't have a telephone, and we received calls at the house of a neighbour, the only person on our block who did. This seems unreal now. We found out about the news mostly from the radio, because there weren't many terrestrial TV channels or national newspapers. There were small papers in each city or town that covered local news. We lived atomised lives, in a fragmented reality, focused only on what went on nearby. Like islands in the middle of nowhere. Some people found it comfortable and safe to live that way, in closed societies where we all knew one another. I found it suffocating. As a girl, I sensed that there wasn't really anywhere I was safe. I'd already seen the signs. At the age of eight, when I was walking to my mum's work one afternoon after church – my mother was a nurse and worked in a clinic a few blocks away – a boy on a bicycle pulled up in front of me and said: Let's fuck! I can clearly remember the knot in my stomach, the way I froze in the middle of the pavement, my eyes filling with tears, unable to say anything or run away. I remember him laughing at my frightened face before riding off on his bicycle. It's not the only example I have, or the worst, but if you've seen one you've seen them all, as my grandmother used to say.

Violence was normalised. The neighbour beaten by her husband, the teenager next door who put up with her jealous boyfriend's tantrums, the father who wouldn't let his daughters wear short skirts or make-up. All the responsibility for what happened to us was laid at our feet: if you stay out late you might be raped, if you talk to strangers you might be raped, if you come back from a dance by yourself you might be raped. If you were raped, it was always your fault.

You could be raped at home as well, but nobody warned you about that. And if it happened and you said something, most likely no one would believe you. The protective family space, a hypocritical Christian concept that nobody questioned.

Maybe that's why Andrea Danne's murder was so shocking: stabbed in her bed, at home, as she slept. Maybe that's why people quickly tried to blame her for her own death. She was young, pretty, desirable and desiring.

Andrea's femicide happened when I was thirteen. Thinking about it now, it was a violent, horrible introduction to adolescence. Being a woman meant being prey. When I was seventeen, in my last year at school, another girl was murdered, in another province. We were the same age. Her name was María Soledad Morales. Unlike all the femicides that were only news in the place where they happened, her story spread throughout the country. It was also the first time there was a Silent March, a means of demanding justice that later became fairly common: a crowd walking through the streets of a city, in total silence. Again they blamed the victim, but this time they also investigated and caught the culprits, with a chain of responsibility that was, of course, made up of men: rich men, the sons of distinguished politicians having fun with lower-middle-class girls; and men from the girls' own social class, who handed them over in exchange for money.

I wrote *Dead Girls* almost thirty years after the femicides of Andrea and María Soledad. At first, the book was going to describe three teenage femicides in the interior of Argentina in the eighties. Stories of women who would now be about my age.

The research (documents, interviews, surveying newspapers from the time; and extensive work with the Señora, a medium, a line of connection to the dead girls) took me three years. Writing the book you now hold in your hands took me three months. The writing process was sustained and painful. As I wrote the stories of Andrea, María Luisa and Sarita, fragments of my own life story and those of women I knew began to work their way in. My friends and I were still alive, but we could have been Andrea, María Luisa or Sarita. We were just luckier.

Selva Almada
Buenos Aires, March 2020

that woman, why is she screaming?
                            who knows
              look at the pretty flowers
             why is she screaming?
hyacinths   *daisies*
                                why?
                          why what?
why is that woman screaming?

Susana Thénon

The morning of November 16th, 1986, was clear and cloudless in Villa Elisa, the town where I was born and raised, in the central eastern part of Entre Ríos province.

It was a Sunday and my dad was grilling meat in the backyard. We still didn't have a proper barbecue, but he made do with a metal sheet on the ground, the coals on top, and a grill on top of the coals. My dad would barbecue in all weathers: if it rained, he just used another piece of metal to cover the meat and the coals.

Near the grill, in the branches of the mulberry tree, a portable, battery-powered radio, tuned permanently to LT26 Radio Nuevo Mundo. They played traditional folk songs and read the news every hour, though there was never much to read. It wasn't yet forest fire season in the El Palmar national park, around thirty miles away, which went up in flames every summer and set off the sirens in all the fire stations nearby. Aside from the odd road accident, always some kid heading back from a dance, barely anything happened at weekends. Not even football in the afternoons, because the heat meant the tournament had moved to the evenings.

I'd been woken that morning in the early hours by a gale that shook the roof of the house. I stretched out in bed and felt something that made me sit bolt upright, heart racing. The mattress was damp, and some warm, slimy forms moved against my legs. Still half-asleep, it took me a few seconds to work out what was going on: my cat had given birth at the foot of the bed again. The lightning that flashed through the window showed her curled up, gazing at me with her yellow eyes. I pulled myself into a ball, hugging my knees, so as not to touch them again.

My sister was asleep in the next bed. The lightning cast a blue glow over her face, her half-open eyes – she always slept that way, like hares do – and her chest as it rose and fell, far removed from the storm and the rain that had swept everything away. I fell asleep too, looking at her.

When I awoke, only my dad was up. My mum, brother and sister were still sleeping. The cat and her kittens had gone from the bed. The only trace of the birth was a yellowish stain with dark edges, at one end of the sheet.

I went out to the yard and told my dad the cat had given birth but I couldn't find her or her kittens. He was sitting in the shade of the mulberry tree, away from the grill but close enough to keep an eye on it. The stainless steel cup he always used was on the ground at his feet, filled with wine and ice. The metal was sweating.

She must've hidden them in the shed, he said.

I looked over, but couldn't bring myself to check. A mad dog we used to have once buried her puppies in the shed. She ripped the head off one of them.

The canopy of the mulberry tree was a green sky with the sun glinting golden through the leaves. In a few weeks it would be covered in fruit, flies would come buzzing around it, the air would be thick with the bitter-sweet smell of overripe mulberries, and no one would want to sit underneath it for a while. But that morning it was beautiful. You just had to watch out for the hairy caterpillars, bright and green like Christmas wreaths, which were sometimes so heavy they fell from the leaves and burned your skin with their acidic sparks.

Then came the news on the radio. I hadn't been paying attention, but I heard every single word.

In the early hours of that same morning, in San José,

a town twelve miles away, a teenager had been murdered in her bed as she slept.

My dad and I remained silent.

From where I stood, I watched him get up from his chair and arrange the coals with a metal rod, levelling them out, bashing them to break up the bigger lumps, his face beaded with sweat from the heat of the flames, the meat he'd just thrown on sizzling gently. A neighbour walked past and shouted something. My dad, still bent over the grill, looked round and waved with his free hand. Be right there, he yelled. And he began nudging the coals aside with the same rod, moving them to one end of the metal, closest to where the ñandubay wood was burning, and leaving just a few, which he figured would be enough to keep the grill hot until he came back. Be right there meant swinging by the bar on the corner for a few cold ones. He slid on the flip-flops that had disappeared in the grass, pulling on the shirt he'd hung from a branch of the mulberry tree.

If you see it going out, shove a few coals back over. I won't be long, he said, hurrying into the street with his sandals flapping, like a kid who's just seen the ice-cream van.

I sat in his chair and picked up the cup he'd left behind. The metal was freezing. An ice cube was floating in the dregs of the wine. I fished it out with two fingers and put it in my mouth to suck. At first it tasted faintly of alcohol, but then it was just water.

When there was only a small piece left, I crunched it between my teeth. I laid one hand on my thigh, below the hem of my shorts. It was a shock to feel it so cold. Like the hand of a corpse, I thought. Not that I'd ever touched one.

I was thirteen, and that morning the news about the dead girl hit me like a revelation. My house, any teenager's house, wasn't really the safest place in the world. You could be killed inside your own home. Horror could live with you, under your roof.

In the days that followed, I learnt more details. The girl's name was Andrea Danne, she was nineteen, blonde, pretty, with blue eyes, she had a boyfriend and was training to be a psychology teacher. Someone had stabbed her in the heart.

For more than twenty years, Andrea was always close by. She returned with the news of every other dead woman. With the names that, in dribs and drabs, reached the front pages of the national press, and steadily mounted up: María Soledad Morales, Gladys McDonald, Elena Arreche, Adriana and Cecilia Barreda, Liliana Tallarico, Ana Fuschini, Sandra Reitier, Carolina Aló, Natalia Melman, Fabiana Gandiaga, María Marta García Belsunce, Marela Martínez, Paulina Lebbos, Nora Dalmasso, Rosana Galliano. Each one made me think of Andrea and her unpunished murder.

One summer, spending a few days in Chaco, a region in the north-east of the country, I came across a story in a local paper. The headline was: Twenty-Five Years Since the Murder of María Luisa Quevedo. A fifteen-year-old girl killed on December 8th, 1983, in the city of Presidencia Roque Sáenz Peña. María Luisa had been missing for several days, and then her raped and strangled body turned up on a patch of wasteland on the outskirts of the city. No one was tried for the murder.

Soon afterwards I also learnt about Sarita Mundín, a girl of twenty, who disappeared on March 12th, 1988, and whose remains were found on December 29th of that year on the banks of the Tcalamochita river, in the town of Villa Nueva, Córdoba province. Another unresolved case.

Three teenage girls from the provinces murdered in the eighties, three unpunished deaths that happened before people in this country even knew the word femicide. That morning I didn't know the name of María Luisa, either, who'd been murdered two years before, or of Sarita Mundín, who was still alive, unaware of what would happen to her in two years' time.

I didn't know a woman could be killed simply for being a woman, but I'd heard stories that gradually, over time, I pieced together. Stories that didn't end in the woman's death, but that saw her subjected to misogyny, abuse and contempt.

I'd heard them from my mother, and there was one in particular that stuck with me. It happened when my mum was very young. She didn't remember the girl's name because she never knew her, but she did remember she lived in La Clarita, a little settlement near Villa Elisa. She was about to get married, and a seamstress in my town was making her wedding dress. She'd come to be measured and to have a couple of fittings, always with her mother, in the family car. For the last fitting she came alone; no one could drive her, so she came by bus. Not used to travelling by herself, she took a wrong turn, and by the time she realised what had happened she was on the road that leads to the cemetery. A road that got very quiet at certain hours of the day. When she saw a car coming, she thought she'd better ask rather than carry on going round in circles, lost. There were four men in the car and they took her with them. She was kidnapped for several days, naked, bound and gagged in what seemed to be a derelict building. They gave her just enough food and water to stay alive, and raped her whenever they felt like it. The girl simply wanted to die. All she could see through the tiny window was sky and fields. One night, she heard the men setting off in a car. She screwed up her courage, managed to untie herself and escaped through the window. She ran across the fields until she came to a house, and the people there helped her. She was never able to identify the place she'd been held captive, or her captors. A few months later, she married her boyfriend.

Another of my mother's stories was more recent, from some two or three years back.

Three guys went to a Saturday dance. One was in love with a girl, the daughter of a traditional Villa Elisa family. She was playing hard to get. Whenever he came after her, she'd let him get close and then give him the slip. This little game of cat and mouse had been going on for months, and the night of the dance was no different. They danced, had a drink, chatted, then she blew him off again. He went to drown his sorrows in the cantina, where his two friends were already several drinks in. It was their idea. Why not wait for her outside the dance and teach her a lesson? The love-struck boy sobered up as soon as he heard them. They were crazy, what the fuck, it was time he went home. The booze was messing with their heads.

But they were serious. These prickteasers needed to be shown. They both left early as well. And they waited on a patch of wasteland by her house. No matter what, the girl would have to pass that way.

She left the dance with a friend. They lived a block apart. Her friend got home first and she carried on, unconcerned, along the route she always took after a dance, in a town where nothing ever happened. They ambushed her in the darkness, beat her, penetrated her, taking it in turns, over and over. And when even their dicks were too disgusted, they went on raping her with a bottle.

From early that morning, the sun was beating down on the metal roof of the Quevedos' house in Monseñor de Carlo, a neighbourhood in Presidencia Roque Sáenz Peña, Chaco. The first days of December gave a taste of the brutal Chaco summer to come, with temperatures in the region often hitting forty degrees. In the torpor of her room, María Luisa opened her eyes and sat up in bed, ready to get up and go to work in the Casucho family home. She'd got a job there not long ago, as a maid.

When dressing, she chose lightweight but pretty clothes. She liked to look nice in the street, though she wore old stuff for work, a shabby t-shirt and skirt, faded from the sun and splattered with bleach. From her poor-girl's wardrobe, she picked out a vest and a floaty cotton skirt, with a little leather belt pulled tight around her waist. She washed her face and brushed her hair, which was medium-length, straight and dark. She shook the aerosol deodorant and sprayed it under her arms, then sprayed a mist over the rest of her body. She floated into the kitchen in that sickly-sweet cloud, drank three or four times from the *mate* gourd her mother prepared her, and left the house.

She'd turned fifteen recently, on October 19th, which that year coincided with Mother's Day. She was a skinny girl, her body still undeveloped. Though fifteen, she could have passed for twelve.

The Casuchos' house was in the centre of Sáenz Peña and María Luisa made the journey, twenty blocks or so, on foot. That morning, December 8th, was the day of the Virgin, a half-holiday. Some of the shops were still open, but the city was quieter than usual, so she wouldn't have seen many people on the way.

She was happy because it was her first job. She started early, around seven, and left at three in the afternoon, after washing the dishes from lunch.

If she'd been planning to stick around in town that afternoon, taking advantage of the holiday, she didn't tell her mother, Ángela Cabral, who, when she saw it was getting dark and María Luisa – Chiqui, as her family called her – still wasn't back from work, began to worry.

Since separating from her husband and the father of her six children, Ángela had lived with her two youngest girls and Yogui, her unmarried son of twenty-seven. He was the man of the house, and his mother turned to him first.

Making the most of his afternoon off, Yogui was at a public swimming pool with some friends. A cousin went to find him there and tell him Ángela was in tears because Chiqui hadn't come home after work.

The first place Yogui tried was their father's house. Oscar Quevedo lived with his new wife, a Bolivian woman his children didn't get on with. But María Luisa wasn't there. The search intensified after that, and as the hours went by it grew more and more frantic.

Neither the witnesses nor the police investigation could ever determine what happened or where the girl was between three o'clock on Thursday December 8th, 1983, when she left work, and the morning of Sunday 11th, when her body was found.

Only Norma Romero and Elena Taborda, two new friends of María Luisa, claimed they saw her after she finished work. They walked a couple of blocks together, but then went their separate ways.

The police search had barely begun when, on the morning of Sunday December 11th, the phone rang in

Police Station 1. Someone was calling to report a body found on a patch of wasteland between Calle 51 and Calle 28, on the outskirts of the city. That area, now abandoned, was where earth used to be extracted for making bricks, and there was still a large, shallow pit that filled with water when it rained, forming a muddy lake the locals call a reservoir. In this almost waterless reservoir, the girl's body was discarded. She'd been strangled with the same leather belt she put on in the morning before leaving for work.

At the same time that Sunday, in Buenos Aires, 687 miles away, the echoes were only just fading from the street parties celebrating the inauguration of Raúl Alfonsín, Argentina's first democratically elected president after seven years of dictatorship. The final stragglers were dozing at bus stops as the buses drove straight past, with not even standing room left.

In Sáenz Peña, everyone had spent Saturday glued to the TV, watching the ceremonies and celebrations live on the National Channel from 8 a.m., when they began. As night fell, they too had gone out to celebrate, in Plaza San Martín, the main square. Those with cars had formed a convoy around the city centre, with mini Argentinian flags fluttering on the aerials, horns honking and passengers hanging out of the windows, waving their arms and singing. Although the elected governor of Chaco, Florencio Tenev, was from the Peronist opposition party and the incoming president was from the centrist Radical party, the return to democracy mattered more than political stripes and no one wanted to be left out of the fun.

While everyone was busy celebrating, the Quevedos went on looking for María Luisa.

The last day Sarita Mundín was seen alive, March 12th 1988, was also a fairly normal one for the girl. She'd been away from Villa María for a few weeks, in the city of Córdoba, looking after her mother in hospital. She'd brought her back to the little apartment on Calle San Martín where she lived with Germán, her four-year-old son, and Mirta, her sister of fourteen, who was pregnant. Their mother had just had an operation and needed taking care of, which would be easier for the Mundín sisters if they all lived in the same place. They crammed in as best they could; the apartment was tiny.

When her lover, Dady Olivero, had helped her rent it, the idea was that just she and Germán would live there, and that Dady could visit easily, without the indiscretion of the city's by-the-hour hotel rooms, which were risky for a married man and well-known entrepreneur. Olivero and his family were the owners of the El Mangrullo meat processing plant.

What with her time in Córdoba and her mother's presence in the apartment, it was a while since Sarita had seen Dady. That day, he said he'd swing by in his car and take her somewhere they could be alone without anyone bothering them.

She didn't want to go anywhere with him. Her relationship with this man, more than ten years her senior and with a family of his own, was petering out. It seems she'd met a guy in Córdoba she was pretty keen on. Still, when Dady came to pick her up that afternoon, despite her lack of enthusiasm, Sarita grabbed a towel – they were going to the river – and a bag, and took the stairs down to the ground floor to meet him.

She hadn't spent as long getting ready as she used to, back when the relationship seemed to be going somewhere and she thought it might change her life. She went out in a long skirt, a t-shirt and flip-flops. Dressed up or not, Sarita was a beautiful woman: slim, with wavy chestnut hair, pale skin, green eyes.

Mirta and Germán followed her onto the pavement. The kid, when he saw his mother heading for the car parked on the kerb, wanted to go with her. But the driver inside said no so sternly that the boy cowered in his aunt's skirt, pouting. Sarita turned round, kissed him and promised to bring him back a present.

But she never returned from that outing.

She was missing for almost a year. At the end of December, the dairy farmer Ubaldo Pérez found the remains of a human skeleton lodged in the branches of a tree, on the banks of the Tcalamochita river, which separates the cities of Villa María and Villa Nueva. They were just outside a place known as La Herradura, next to Villa Nueva. The state of the remains – bare bones – suggests she was killed on the same day she went out with her lover, though it was never possible to say how.

When I started university I moved with a friend to Paraná, the provincial capital, a hundred and twenty-five miles from my town. We lived in a boarding house and money was tight. To save cash, we started hitchhiking at weekends when we went to visit our families. At first we always tried to find a guy we knew, another student, to go with us. Then we realised we got picked up more quickly as just girls. In pairs or threes it didn't feel dangerous. And eventually, as we grew more confident, we each took to travelling alone if we couldn't find another girl to join us. Sometimes exams meant we didn't go back to our hometown on the same day. We got into cars, lorries, trucks. We didn't get in if there was more than one man in the vehicle, but other than that, we didn't take many precautions.

In five years, I went there and back hundreds of times without paying for a ticket. Hitchhiking was the cheapest way of getting around, and sometimes it was even interesting. You'd meet people. You'd chat. Mostly, you'd listen: the lorry drivers in particular, tired of their lonely work, would tell us their entire life stories as we added fresh hot water to their *mate*.

There was the odd uncomfortable incident. One time a lorry driver from Mendoza, while telling me his troubles, said that female students sometimes slept with him to make a few pesos and that he saw nothing wrong with it, it was a way of paying for their studies and helping their parents out. It never went beyond this insinuation, but for the rest of the journey I felt very uneasy. Whenever I got into a car, the first thing I did was check where the inside lock was. I think that day I slid over the seat until I was pressed against the window, and kept hold of the handle in case I had to make a break for it. Another time, a young guy in a fancy car, who was driving too fast, told me he was a gynaecologist and started explaining about the regular check-ups a woman should have, the importance of detecting tumours, of catching cancer in time. He asked if I went for check-ups. I said yes, of course, every year, even though it wasn't true. And while he was talking and driving he reached out a hand and started fondling my tits. I froze, the seatbelt across my chest. Without taking his eyes off the road, the guy said: You can spot any suspicious lumps you might have on your own, touching yourself like this, see.

However, only once did I feel we were in real danger. A friend and I were travelling from Villa Elisa to Paraná, one Sunday afternoon. It had been a difficult journey, with a lot of stopping and starting. We got into and out of a whole series of cars and lorries. The last one left us at a crossroads near Viale, around forty miles from Paraná.

It was getting dark and there wasn't a soul on the road. Finally we saw a car approaching. An orange car, neither new nor old. We flagged it down and the driver pulled over. We ran a few yards to catch up. It was going to Paraná, so we got in, my friend next to the man at the wheel, a guy of around sixty, and me in the back. For the first couple of miles we covered all the usual topics: the weather, where we were from, what we studied. The man told us he was on his way home from some farmland he had in the area. I couldn't hear very well from the back, and since my friend seemed to have the conversation in hand, I settled into my seat and looked out of the window. I don't know how long it was before I realised something strange was going on. Instead of watching the road, the guy was leaning in to talk to my friend, and he seemed more animated than before. I sat up a bit. Then I saw his hand patting her knee, and the same hand moving upwards and stroking her arm. I started chattering away about whatever came into my head: the state of the road, the exams we had that week. But the guy took no notice. He went on talking to my friend, inviting her to go for a drink when we arrived. She didn't lose her cool or stop smiling, but I knew that deep down she was as frightened as me. No, thanks, I've got a boyfriend. Why should I care, I'm not jealous. I bet your boyfriend's just a kid, what can he teach you about life. A girl like you needs a mature man like me. Protection. Financial security. Experience. The phrases reached me in bits. Outside, night had fallen and you couldn't even see the fields by the roadside. I looked all around: everything was black. And when I spotted the guns lying on the shelf behind my seat, my blood ran cold. They were two long guns, rifles or something.

My friend went on deflecting the man's persistent advances, pleasantly and calmly, dodging his arm as he tried to grab hold of her wrist. I was talking non-stop, though no one was paying attention. Talking and talking and talking, and I never normally talk – an act of infinite desperation.

Then the same thing that had made my blood run cold returned it to my body. I was closer to the guns than he was. Not that I'd ever used one.

Finally, the lights at the entrance to the city. The petrol station where we could get the bus into the centre. We asked him to drop us there. The guy sneered at us, pulled over and came to a halt: Yes, get out why don't you, silly little bitches.

We got out and walked to the bus stop. The orange car started up and drove off. When it was a long way away, we dropped our bags, hugged each other and burst into tears.

Maybe María Luisa and Sarita felt lost in the moments before they died. But Andrea Danne was asleep when she was stabbed, on November 16th, 1986.

That Saturday had been like all the other Saturdays for the past year and a half, since she'd started dating Eduardo. It had finished quite a bit earlier, without them going to a dance or a motel like they sometimes did. The following Monday Andrea would have the first of her final exams to qualify as a psychology teacher, which she'd started training for that year. She was nervous and not feeling very confident, and wanted to get an early night and study in bed for a bit instead of going out with her boyfriend.

They spent a few hours together, though, when he came by on his motorbike to see her. They drank *mate* and talked, sitting on the pavement; it was a boiling hot day and a storm was brewing.

The sun had disappeared behind the low houses in the neighbourhood, and the few street lamps on Calle Centenario were lighting up and filling with bugs. The sprinkler truck drove by, damping down the dust in the road and leaving the pavements steaming and smelling of rain.

At around nine they headed into the kitchen, made some *milanesa* sandwiches, poured cold drinks and went back to the pavement. The house was small, and when her parents and brother were in as well, there was more privacy outside than indoors.

While they were eating, Fabiana, Andrea's sister, appeared and asked her to help choose an outfit for the dance that night. It was Noche de las Quinceañeras at the Santa Rosa club, which had become a tradition in the city of San José: all the girls who'd turned fifteen that year paraded up and down in their dresses and everyone chose the prettiest.

So the sisters went indoors, and Eduardo was left finishing his sandwich by himself.

The neighbours were bringing chairs outside and some had turned their TVs to face the pavement, with the volume up high so they could hear them over the street noise: a few cars, but mostly groups of kids playing tag or catching fireflies. There was no cable back then. TVs used aerials and only Channel 7 from Buenos Aires and Channel 3 from Paysandú reached that area, so everyone watched more or less the same shows. The scent of the mosquito spirals soon filled the air.

Later, Andrea and Eduardo went for a ride around the centre on his motorbike. The traffic built up near the main square, with lots of cars and motorbikes cruising along, as if in a procession. They had an ice cream and then went back to Andrea's.

Her parents and brother were in bed; Fabiana had gone to the dance. The house was silent, the sound of the TV in her parents' bedroom barely filtering through the thin walls. The kids spent a while making out in the kitchen. At one point they heard noises in the yard. Eduardo went out to have a look and didn't see anything unusual, but the way the wind was moving the treetops and the neighbours' clothes on the line warned him the weather was turning. He said as much to his girlfriend when he went back indoors and they decided he should go, so he wasn't caught in the storm. He didn't set off right away. They kissed some more, touching each other under their clothes, until she put her foot down: time for him to leave.

She went with him as far as the street. The wind made her long blonde hair billow around and her clothes cling to her body. They kissed one last time, he started the engine and she hurried inside.

She left the window to the yard open. Although the temperature had dropped a little, the walls were still hot and the sheets warm, as if freshly ironed. She lay in bed, in her vest and knickers, and picked up some papers, stapled and underlined photocopies with her handwritten notes in the margins.

However, she must have dozed off before long. According to her mother's statement, when the wind picked up and she went in to close the window, Andrea was already asleep. It was past midnight. She finished watching a film they were showing on *Private Function*, a classic program from the eighties presented by Carlos Morelli and Rómulo Berruti. They showed a film, and when it finished the two presenters discussed it over glasses of whisky. That night it was *Marijuana Smoke*, from around twenty years earlier, directed by Lucas Demare. The film didn't interest her, but since she wasn't tired she watched it to the end. Then she turned off the TV, not waiting to hear Morelli and Berruti's comments, and managed to drift off.

After a bit she woke up, got out of bed, went to her daughters' bedroom and switched on the light. Andrea was still in bed, but she had a bloody nose. The mother says she was paralysed, didn't move from the doorway and shouted for her husband, two or three times.

Come here, something's happened to Andrea.

He paused to pull on some trousers and a work shirt before going into the bedroom. When he lifted Andrea up by the shoulders, a little more blood trickled from her chest.

The other bed, Fabiana's, was still empty and made up. The storm had reached its glorious climax. The wild gusts of wind merged with the rain, and the zinc roof made a noise like gunfire.

Andrea must have felt lost when she woke up to die. Her eyes, suddenly open, would have blinked a few times in the two or three minutes it took her brain to run out of oxygen. Lost, dazed by the drumming of the rain and the wind that snapped the thinnest branches of the trees in the yard, hazy with sleep, utterly disoriented.

The Quevedos, after reporting their sister's disappearance to the police and being met with the usual response – that they should wait, that she must have gone off with a boyfriend and would be back in no time – decided to consult a psychic. A Paraguayan woman, who saw people in a modest little house. The large patio, which ran right up to the street, accommodated the visitors and their woes. They piled in, jostling for the meagre shade under the trees with some dogs that were always hanging around.

Despite setting out more or less at sunrise, they found plenty of people waiting by the time they arrived. One of the Paraguayan's assistants, whose job it was to keep the crowd in order and deal with the fights that broke out whenever some chancer tried to push in, approached them and asked what they'd come about. They explained. The assistant listened carefully to everything they said and then went into the hut. He emerged right away and beckoned them over. She'll see you now, he said, leaning in slightly and whispering to avoid the complaints, which came regardless when they were spotted going in first despite being the last to arrive.

The psychic didn't tell them much: only that yes, she would come back, that it was Friday now and by Sunday it would all be over.

Eduardo, Andrea's boyfriend, also decided to consult a psychic. Two, in fact. The first somewhat by chance, because the man came to buy a few things from his family's shop. A little sheepishly, Eduardo took him to one side, over by some shelves, and asked if he could look into his girlfriend's death. The man stared deep into his eyes, horrified, and told him he didn't mess with the devil's business.

Later, one of Andrea's cousins had the idea they should consult another: Luis Danta, who was a very famous psychic back then and saw people in Paysandú, a Uruguayan city some twelve miles from Colón, where Eduardo lived. Many people crossed the General Artigas international bridge every day to see Danta.

They went on the motorbike.

After you cross the bridge, the greenery by the roadside turns to riverside plants, because of the wetlands that reach almost to the tarmac.

Eduardo was riding at full speed, Andrea's cousin clinging round his waist. Neither was wearing a helmet – back then almost nobody did. His long hair kept hitting her in the face, forcing her to squint and surrender to the power of the machine. Their visit to the healer hadn't given them any answers. Just ambiguous phrases, here and there in the trance. Eduardo was thinking about Andrea, thinking about her was all he ever did, and about solving the mystery of her death. Hence the speed, too, he was like a madman, nothing mattered, if he had to be killed in a crash so be it, maybe that would bring some peace to his heart and head, and his endless questions: who, why.

Just before they crossed back from the Uruguayan side of the bridge, a jararaca viper almost two metres long appeared suddenly in the middle of the road. The creature was half-coiled on the tarmac, though as the bike got closer Eduardo thought he saw it rear up, ready to spring and attack. The thick body, pale brown with dark patches, and the pale speckled belly, glittered in the sun. He swerved instinctively to avoid running it over, and he and Andrea's cousin were almost flung onto the scorching road. He'd always imagined dying that way, but what shook him was seeing the jararaca in their path after the first psychic had talked of the devil's business. He took the encounter with the snake as a sign.

When I was little, my grandma and I also used to go to a healer, Old Man Rodríguez. He lived in a shack on the edge of town, near a poor neighbourhood called Tiro Federal.

It made me nervous, but at the same time I liked going to his house and didn't mind having to traipse all the way across town, always with a sore head or stomach, because if my grandma was taking me it was because I had indigestion or worms. I found the Old Man a bit frightening. He was very thin, as if his own body were sucking at his flesh from the inside, and this made him stoop, his skin shrunken like a freshly washed shirt. I don't remember his face, but I do remember he had long fingernails like a woman's. Dirty and yellow, his emaciated claws would slide over my swollen belly, tracing the shape of a cross a few times while he murmured things I didn't understand.

His very gauntness made him look holy.

The room where he saw people was small and dark, badly ventilated. The flames of the candles burning here and there, always in different places, showed only a fraction of the room, which was whitewashed to ward off the vermin. I never had a full sense of what that room was like or what furniture there was, and I never recognised the faces in the prints on the walls or clustered atop the little makeshift altar.

He lived alone and on what we gave him. Sometimes cash, sometimes *yerba mate*, sugar, spaghetti, sometimes a piece of meat.

As well as curing parasites and indigestion, Old Man Rodríguez knew the secret of burns, sprains, shingles and even *pata de cabra*, that disease which can eat away at a baby and boil it in its own stomach juices.

I don't know where his powers came from. Whether he'd inherited them from his mother or whether he'd been born with them, like a blessing that every now and then became a curse. When his powers took a dark turn, the Old Man wouldn't answer even if people beat down his door, even if hordes of children were crying outside and the mothers were begging to be let in. Inside, most likely flat out on his camp bed, the Old Man would sleep off his drinking binge, taking a break from his secrets and powers, his body unconscious after the battering from bad wine, his mind blank. On those days there was no point waiting in the sun for night to fall. We could only turn back, insides crawling with worms, stomachs like drums, heads muddled.

Rodríguez the healer died long ago, in a bed in San Roque hospital, where old people who are alone in the world, with no family and no money, end their days. He would have had a pauper's funeral, his body placed in an unsanded, unvarnished coffin, badly made and with no bronze handles, because why bother if there were no mourners to lift it. A casket barely stronger than an apple crate. He can't have weighed much, the poor guy. Without a prayer for his soul or a priestly blessing, since there's no mercy for those who know the secret, those whose powers offend God. He'd have been buried in an out-of-the-way plot, right up against the wire fence separating the cemetery from the neighbouring fields, barbed wire to stop the cows getting through and nibbling the stems of the flowers that wilt in the vases on summer days. An out-of-the-way plot, where people are buried when they have no one.

I come to the Señora on the recommendation of some writer friends who consult her when they have to make important decisions. They trust her sound judgement and her tarot cards.

When I call to ask for an appointment, I explain that my request might seem unusual: I don't want to see her on my own behalf, but on behalf of three women who are dead. She tells me it's more common than I think, and we agree a day and time.

No one's ever done a card reading for me before and I'm slightly nervous at the thought. I'm worried she hasn't understood that it's not me I want to find out about but María Luisa, Andrea and Sarita. I don't want to know my future. I don't want her to dredge up any festering trauma from my past.

I felt confident when I went to Old Man Rodríguez because I was going there to be cured, but the gypsies terrified me because they could see the future. Every now and then they stopped in our town, on the same area of waste ground used by circuses and funfairs. They put up a big tent under the eucalyptus trees that surrounded the field, almost on the tarmac road known as Tráfico Pesado – for heavy vehicles – which joins Avenida Urquiza and then Avenida 131, to Villaguay. They made a living buying and selling cars. By the tent, along the roadside, they parked a line of cars and trucks, which displayed their chrome paintwork, gleaming in the sun, to everyone who passed.

In the weeks and even months they camped there, you'd often come across the women out shopping or walking around the town. Always in pairs or threes, sometimes with small children in tow, wearing those flowing gauze skirts and with scarves partly covering their very long, loose or plaited hair, their arms a mass of golden bracelets, their ears heavy with those golden hoops, and their feet clad in high-heeled shoes. No one trusted them: when they went into the grocer's and other shops, an employee always watched them closely because everyone said their fingers were lightning quick. People said they stole children, too, that they snatched them away and sold them in the next town where they camped. They seemed to find all this suspicion entertaining. Whenever they walked past anyone, they'd shout out an offer to read their palm. That was what I found so terrifying, that they might grab my hand just like that, turn it over and read everything my palm could tell them, right down to the day of my death.

Once I saw something that made me look at these women differently. I'd been out running errands, I must have been around ten, and some way off I saw a gypsy couple. You didn't often see the men in the street like that. It seemed they'd come out of a shop and were arguing on the pavement. He was waving his arms around, and as I got closer I heard him yelling. I kept at a safe distance, pretending to look in a shop window, because I was scared to walk too close to them. Out of the corner of my eye, I went on observing the scene. The man, a young guy, was talking very loudly, in a language I didn't understand. She was listening to him, head bowed. At one point he shoved her in the shoulder. The woman's body was thrown slightly off balance, but she didn't fall. He turned and marched off with long, determined strides. Instead of following him, and I think he was expecting her to follow him, the woman sat down on the kerb and stayed there for who knows how long. I watched him vanish into the distance and grew tired of waiting for her to get up and leave. I screwed up my courage and walked straight past, behind her. She was hunched over, staring at her knees, and using a twig to draw in the loose dirt that had gathered by the roadside.

The Señora is a slim woman, with long, black hair and a blunt fringe. She wears miniskirts, and her lips and finger-nails are painted red. She has tattoos. She must be around my mother's age, but she looks like a young girl. As we go up the two flights of stairs, we talk about our mutual acquaintances. In her studio, she waves me towards a very comfortable chair, with wooden armrests and soft uphol-stery. She opens the windows slightly. The studio is built on the flat roof and has rectangular windows running all along two walls, and glass on the third through which cacti in pots can be seen dotted here and there on the brick-red tiles. She sits in a similar chair to mine, though hers looks more like a throne: a fair bit larger and made of wicker. A coffee table stands between us. There's nothing on top but a green cloth folded in two.

I repeat what I told her over the phone and reveal a little more: in two of the cases the relatives consulted psychics, but pretty much nothing came of those experi-ences. Maybe it was too soon, and maybe now it's too late, I venture.

It's never too late. But I think everything in the next world is tangled up together, like a ball of wool. You have to be patient and keep tugging at the end, a little at a time. Do you know the story of the Bone Woman?

I shake my head.

She's an old, old woman and she lives deep in her lair of lairs. A wild old woman who clucks like a hen, sings like a bird and makes noises that are more animal than human. Her task is gathering bones. She collects and looks after everything that's in danger of being lost. Her hut is full of all kinds of animal bones, but wolf bones are her favourite. She'll cover miles and miles, scale mountains, wade through streams, burn the soles of her feet on desert sands to find them. Back in her hut, with her armful of bones, she pieces together the skeleton. When the final to hit her, and that he knew how to do it so you never saw the marks. No one reported it. After her death, word got around that he'd killed her and covered it up, making it look like a suicide. It was possible. It was also possible that she'd hanged herself, sick of the life she was leading.

And it was there when we talked about the wife of López the butcher. Her daughters went to my school. She reported him for rape. For some time, as well as beating her up, he'd been sexually abusing her. I was twelve years old, and this news made a big impression on me. How could her husband have raped her? Rapists were always unknown men who grabbed hold of a woman and dragged her off to some patch of wasteland, or who broke into her house by forcing a door. From a very young age, we girls were told not to speak to strangers, and to watch out for the Satyr. The Satyr, in those early childhood years, was a figure as magical as the child-snatching Solapa or the Sack Man. It was the Satyr who could rape you if you went out alone at the wrong time or strayed into desolate places. Who could appear out of nowhere and carry you off to some building site. They never told us you could be raped by your husband, your dad, your brother, your cousin, your neighbour, your granddad, your teacher. A man you trusted completely.

And it was there when Cachito García would disturb the whole neighbourhood's siestas by yelling at his girlfriend. Cachito was a petty thief and he was dating the eldest daughter of our neighbours the Bonnots. Don Bonnot worked building roads and was away from home most of the year. His wife and numerous female offspring, all very pretty girls, lived by themselves. Cachito, a jealous guy, was forever having a go at his girlfriend because she wore make-up or tight clothes or he saw her talking to another guy. One time he went a bit further. The Bonnot house was a wooden prefab and Cachito sprinkled the sides with kerosene and threatened to set it alight. The neighbours stopped him before everything went up in flames.

Alongside these situations sat other, more minor examples. My friend's mum, who never wore make-up because her husband wouldn't let her. My mother's colleague, who handed her whole salary over to her husband each month to take care of. The woman who couldn't see her family because her husband looked down on them. The woman who wasn't allowed to wear high heels because they were for whores.

I grew up hearing grown women discussing situations like these in whispers, as if they were embarrassed by the poor woman's plight, or as if they too were afraid of the man who hit her.

My mother discussed these stories loudly, indignantly, and it was always her fellow gossiper who signalled for her to lower her voice, or who gestured at us children, murmuring in the usual code: Careful, there's laundry hanging up... as if saying those things were like saying dirty words, or worse, as if they were a source of unimaginable shame.

Mirta, Sarita Mundín's sister, suspects that Dady Olivero used to hit her. Sarita never told her outright, but she was scared of him. In private, the two of them used to call Olivero the Randy Pig. Towards the end, whenever she knew he was coming over, Sarita would fill the house with her friends, guys and girls her age, so she didn't have to be alone with him. Olivero would hang around for a bit, hiding his annoyance, drink a few *mates* and then leave in a huff.

The last day she spent with her sister, as if Sarita knew it was the last and wanted to teach her something that would stay with her, they had a conversation that Mirta will never forget.

Her sister told her: Don't let anyone push you around. You have to make people respect you. Never let a guy lay a finger on you. If they hit you once, they'll hit you forever.

Sarita was pregnant when she got married at fifteen. Mirta was following in her footsteps, single and expecting a baby at fourteen. Soon after Germán was born, Sarita's husband started demanding she bring in some cash. Sarita turned to prostitution. She was picked up by Olivero, who would be first her customer, then her lover and protector, and the last person she was ever seen with.

From hustling by the roadside, she went on to build up a client list among the local branch of the Radical party. She and her friend Miriam García were party activists, two pretty young girls who soon caught the eye of the elderly men, distinguished members of society with the hypocrisy to match. Perhaps because of her fresh, girlish appearance, she was a hit with the old guys. But although things were going pretty well with the Radicals, and she had Olivero's protection, too, there was one customer Sarita didn't stop visiting. Another elderly, single man who lived in Oncativo, a city forty miles from Villa María, and who, according to Miriam García, helped her out with money.

José Bertoni, a bachelor uncle of my mother's, also had a woman, La Chola, who visited him at home. José owned a dumper truck and transported sand and stones short distances from a nearby quarry. He lived in a very nice house that he'd built himself. My cousin and I always went there to play because he had a huge garden with swings and because he let us do whatever we liked. Some afternoons, we'd see La Chola turn up with three or four kids around our age. She went inside with my uncle and we carried on playing. We knew that on no account were we to go inside or call them while they were in there. After a while they came out and had some *mate*, and La Chola fixed us a snack.

One of her children was a girl not much older than me. I don't remember her name, but I do remember she was pretty and turned into a little woman overnight, with large breasts and wide hips that stretched the child's dresses she still wore. And that on one of those afternoons she was the one who went inside with José Bertoni, while La Chola stayed on the patio drinking *mate* and we carried on playing as if nothing was going on.

Visiting a single man who slips you some cash in return is a kind of prostitution that's normalised in provincial towns. Like the maid who meets her employer's husband out of hours to add a few pesos to her salary. I saw it with girls in my family, when I was little. In the night, from the street, you hear a car horn. She's been waiting, she grabs her purse and hurries out. No one asks any questions.

After Sarita's disappearance, Olivero went on visiting the family. He took them cash, and packets of meat from his processing plant. Although the mother suspected he'd been mixed up in what happened, that he'd done something to her daughter, she accepted the gifts, swallowing her fury and pride. They were so poor that sometimes they had nothing to eat. Mirta was pregnant and they were raising Sarita's son. The mouths needed feeding somehow.

It was Mirta who put a stop to Olivero's charity visits. That last conversation with her sister was what gave her the courage to call time, on the afternoon when the Randy Pig showed up with the packets of meat and asked her to step into Sarita's shoes.

Of the three towns where the girls were born, grew up and were murdered, I only know one from back then: San José. I remember it from my childhood and teenage years, as an obligatory stop between my town and the city of Colón, where my aunt lived. I only ever saw San José through the bus window. We never got out or walked around, there was no reason to because we didn't know anyone who lived there. But it struck me as an ugly, uninspiring place.

As soon as you entered the town you had to go past the Vizental meat plant. Its high chimneys were always smoking, day and night, filling the whole town with the greasy, pestilent stench of cooking meat, skin and bones. If we went by very, very early in the morning, I liked to look at the plant workers we passed on the way: they were going in the opposite direction to us, men and women on bicycles, dressed all in white from head to toe. There was something strange and unreal about those cyclists pedalling slowly along the side of the road, wreathed in the dirty morning light. Now and then it looked like they were floating: a legion of ghosts.

There were rumours in the area about people from San José: that they practised black magic, that they were always getting into fights, that the guys went everywhere with a knife in their belt and all the women were easy. Comments from towns where most people were farmers with European heritage. San José was a factory town, almost everyone lived off the meat plant in some way. In its neighbours' imaginations, it was as if the stinking black smoke from the Vizental also contaminated the lives and customs of the residents. They were workers and they were poor, they spent their days butchering cows, hacking them up, cooking them, and then putting them in tins that were sold in supermarkets all over the country. Whereas we sowed, harvested, worked the land. Our air was clean and pure, barely tainted, now and then, by the smell of petrol from the threshing machines. If people from San José showed up at the dances in Villa Elisa or Colón, sooner or later there'd be a skirmish. Not because they directly provoked it, but because, for us, the presence of these undesirable neighbours at any of our gatherings was provocation enough.

When people heard the news of Andrea's murder, it was as if all those prejudices found their vindication. No one seemed surprised that such a brutal murder had happened there. Soon people were talking about cults, satanic rituals, witchcraft.

Still, there is something ritualistic about the way she was murdered: stabbed once in the heart, while she slept. As if her own bed were the sacrificial stone.

Tacho Zucco is a sculptor and lives in Chajarí, the most north-easterly part of Entre Ríos province, in a house he built with his own hands. A simple, cosy house, with big windows that overlook the courtyard, and that let in all the light on a sunny Sunday. Now that his four children are studying in Buenos Aires, the only people left in the house are him and Silvia, his wife. The same person who was his girlfriend and expecting a baby when Andrea was killed. Tacho and the dead girl were good friends.

A couple of years before the murder, he moved to San José, where he opened a record shop and got to know Andrea and her sister and their group of friends. In no time the shop had attracted all the young people in San José and alarmed many of the adults. Tacho Zucco was the guy from out of town who brought in those rock cassettes, and teenagers would hang out in his shop and smoke weed. He's surprised when I tell him his name comes up a lot in the case file. It's because they found some letters from him among Andrea's things.

He thought she was gorgeous, but nothing ever happened between them. He wouldn't have wanted to be her boyfriend because her boyfriends had such a hard time of it; she was somehow both there and not there, she never fully committed, never let herself go. She was like that with everything, he remembers. As if she were always floating somewhere between the earth and the sky.

In the year and a bit that he lived in San José, he never felt comfortable. The town was very different to Chajarí. Everything was darker, murkier.

The kids had this thing they did, this game, I don't know what the word is, he tells me. They called it calving. They'd pick out a girl, always someone lower-class. One of the group would make like he was her boyfriend. He'd follow her down the street, say stuff to her, try to seduce her. This would be during the week, and it couldn't take too long: the calving happened at the weekend, so the conquest had to be quick. Once the girl yielded, an invitation would follow to the Saturday dance. But first a drink in the café, and then a spin in the car. They never made it to the dance. The car would veer off towards the riverbank or some other deserted spot. There the rest of the gang would be waiting, and the girl had to do it with everyone. They passed her round everyone, more like. Then they gave her some cash so she didn't squeal. I'd never heard of anything like that here in Chajarí.

Although there was a case a while back that reminded me of the calf thing.

Zucco is talking about the murder of Alejandra Martínez, a girl of seventeen who disappeared in the early hours of one morning in May 1998, outside a nightclub, and who reappeared one month later, dead. Her body was left in Colonia Belgrano, six miles from Chajarí, on some land bordered by eucalyptus trees, partly hidden under a pile of timber. She was found by a farm labourer who'd gone in there looking for a lost animal. She was semi-naked and in an advanced state of decomposition, her nipples had been cut off and her vagina and uterus removed, along with most of her fingertips. Some witnesses said they'd seen her in the neighbourhood at six that morning, others that a group of guys had bundled her into a taxi, and one neighbour said she heard someone shouting for help and shortly after saw the girl's father-in-law loading something heavy into his car outside the house and driving away. The father-in-law was held for two years on suspicion of the crime, though there was never any concrete proof against him and in the end the case was dismissed and they let him go. In the eyes of the Chajarí residents, who organised various silent marches demanding justice for Alejandra, the father-in-law was a scapegoat: rumours had long connected the case to a private party involving the sons of politicians and police officers.

Zucco's wife brews some more *mate*. She says word got around that the son of a famous surgeon was mixed up in Alejandra Martínez' murder, and that it was the father who'd cut her open and removed the organs, though to what end she doesn't know, whether to disguise a rape, destroy the evidence or what. And that they'd stored her in a freezer for several days before discarding her body in the wasteland; they'd kept her on ice while they decided what to do.

She doesn't have fond memories of San José either. When she visited Tacho and went out with the girls or chatted to them, there were some things she couldn't get used to.

It might sound silly now. But I remember that was when thongs had just come into fashion. And for example, a girl in the group had bought one and she used to share it with everyone else. If one of them had a date that night, she'd ask her friend for the thong. See what I mean? I wasn't into that stuff. The whole time, it all felt kind of sleazy. Although really I was a bit jealous, too, because Tacho was their friend and I felt like a prude, she says with a laugh.

Since Tacho had closed the record shop and moved back to Chajarí, it was a few days before they heard about Andrea's death. Someone mentioned it, but without saying how she'd died, and he imagined a heart attack, something sudden, tragic, but a death by natural causes. He travelled back to see Fabiana and the group of friends he'd made in those months. As soon as he got off the bus, he ran into a girl he knew at the terminal and she told him the details. From that day on, he never again set foot in the town. He never spoke to Fabiana again, or any of the rest of the gang.

In the case file, these details are described as follows:

On a wooden bed 190cm long, 90cm wide and 50cm high, which is set against the wall on the west side of the room, with the head of the bed towards the south wall and touching both walls, the body of Miss María Andrea

Danne lies face-up, head turned slightly to the right, resting on the pillow, with a considerable amount of blood on the chest, sheet, mattress and part of the bed, specifically the spring on the right side, and a pool of blood on the floor to the right of the bed. The above-mentioned girl is lifeless, covered to the waist by a sheet and a quilt, both hands resting on her stomach, and wearing a red vest, stained with her own blood, and bikini briefs. One brown leather sandal is visible under the bed, and, next to the bed, the second of the pair, these presumably being the shoes the victim was wearing. There is no sign of the bedclothes being disordered, that is, there are no signs of struggle, the hair of the deceased is neat and tidy.

Tacho Zucco doesn't know who could have killed her, or why. When I tell him that in the city's collective unconscious, the murderers are Andrea's parents, he looks at me, surprised. More than surprised, visibly shaken.

Later – we've already said goodbye and I'm in a taxi on the way to the bus terminal – he sends me a text: The story of Abraham and Isaac, I can't believe it.

Again, this idea of sacrifice.

The first time I spoke to Yogui Quevedo, the brother who was living with María Luisa when she was murdered, I did so from Buenos Aires. A journalist from Sáenz Peña gave me his mobile number. The connection was poor and kept cutting out. I went onto the patio to see if it improved. A little, but not enough. I asked him to go outside as well, and then we did manage to speak more easily. Yogui was standing on the pavement. The signal was more even, but now the interruptions came when every so often someone greeted him and he responded.

The thing is, everyone knows me round here, he said.

It was a few months before I could travel to Chaco to interview him. I have family in Villa Ángela, a city sixty miles from Sáenz Peña. A couple of years earlier, in the very house where I'm going to stay, I read the newspaper article that led me to María Luisa.

As soon as I'm settled in, I call and we arrange to meet the next afternoon. His instructions take me by surprise, but I agree to them. When I'm approaching Sáenz Peña in the bus that afternoon, I'm to send him a text message and he'll tell me where to meet.

I send the first message as we drive under the metal arch that says Welcome to Thermal City. The second when I reach the bus station. I step down onto a platform where one lot of people are waiting for their bus and another lot are waiting for the people who've just arrived. Like most provincial bus terminals, it's grubby and neglected.

I look at the men waiting for passengers to see if I can spot Yogui, though I've never seen a photo of him. Nothing. The people waiting with anxious faces begin to smile as they hug the new arrivals and offer help with bags and cases. The platform is emptying and I stay near the bus, just in case, until the luggage man closes the hold and the vehicle reverses, leaving the bay free for the next one.

I need to pee, but I'm scared he'll turn up when I'm in the bathroom. So I send another message: I'm here, I'm going to the bathroom, wait for me.

In the bathroom, a woman sitting at a little table is handing out pieces of folded toilet roll and paper towels. There's a strong smell of disinfectant and it's very hot. Women go in and out of the cubicles, there's a queue. When it's finally my turn, I step into the cubicle but there's no water in the toilet bowl.

Just a trickle comes out of the tap in the sink. I wet my fingertips, like in a baptismal font, and walk out without taking a paper towel.

Of course, Yogui Quevedo isn't waiting for me. I call him. The voicemail picks up. I leave a message. I wait. I call again. I call five more times in the next half-hour. Suddenly I remember that, in our extremely brief exchange a while back, he said his brothers had a travel agency. I go into a call shop and ask for a directory, then write down an address and get in a taxi.

When I walk into the tour agency, the young man at the desk greets me with a smile. He must think I'm a potential customer. When I explain that I don't want to buy a package holiday and tell him the real reason I'm sitting opposite him, he looks deflated and I feel bad. Even though I've disappointed him, he carries on being friendly. A few blocks from there, some kids have an agency that runs shopping tours, that must be what I'm after, though he's not sure if their surname is Quevedo.

I thank him and head back into the street, where the air is thick and heavy.

The place I end up looks nothing like the glass-fronted office decorated with pictures of sublime landscapes I've just left. This one is on the ground floor of a crumbling two-storey building, with broken windows covered by pieces of cardboard. Later I learn that the building belongs to Carlos Janik, one of the forensic scientists who worked on the Quevedo case. I'd written to Janik a few months back, hoping to interview him, and he'd answered that not only did he have no recollection of the case but he also had no idea what had become of the girl's family, and so couldn't put me in touch with them.

The office is closed, and although I ring the bell and knock on the door, the only response is the barking of a neighbour's dog. Outside there's a board that reads Trips to Bolivia and La Salada. With a mobile number. I dial. It rings a couple of times and a man picks up.

I tell him why I'm phoning and he says his brother should be in the office, that if he's not there he doesn't know where he could be, that he doesn't know where he lives these days. That as for him, he's in Bolivia with a tour group, and has to hang up because he's driving.

Phone in hand, I sit on a brick wall that runs along the edge of the pavement. I take a deep breath and try Quevedo's number one more time. Again, the voicemail says: He's not available, please leave a message after the tone. I leave a final terse message, not bothering to hide my annoyance.

I go back to the station and buy a ticket for the next bus to Villa Ángela. Luckily it's just about to leave. I resign myself to another two and a half hours on a dilapidated bus (yes, it took me two and a half hours to get there, two and a half hours for a journey of sixty miles), which has no toilet, no air conditioning, and stops every five minutes, the kind that in the interior of the country we call milk floats.

As soon as they let us on, I look for a window seat so I can at least watch the scenery go by and breathe the hot air from the road. Foam oozes from the rips in the fake leather seat, which won't recline because the mechanism's jammed. The bus soon fills up, but the seat next to me stays empty. I think perhaps the good luck I didn't have all afternoon is finally kicking in and I'll travel with no one beside me.

The bus jolts backwards and we're out of the bay, it turns and we exit the terminal. Until we finally leave the city behind, it will stop every block or two, even twice on the same block, to pick up the passengers who wait, without rhyme or reason, at the point on the block where they've put down their bag, without taking another step even if there are more passengers just fifty yards away, most likely waiting for this same bus.

A stocky blonde girl gets on at one of the stops, clutching various bags. She edges sideways down the aisle and then drops into the seat next to mine. She's seriously huge, of Eastern European descent like so many people in the region. I squeeze over as far as I can against the window and open it as wide as it'll go. The girl's sickly-sweet perfume is making me dizzy. And the journey has only just begun.

I take short deep breaths and try to think of something else.

Jesús Gómez, who María Luisa's family identify as her murderer, was the owner of a bus company like this one. Thirty years ago his fleet of coaches drove all over the province, connecting cities and small towns.

A former driver with the company, who was also friends with Gómez, tells me he was something of a womaniser, even then, when he was past seventy.

He was a bit too partial to the really young girls, everyone knew it. His own staff used to fix him up with them for cash.

In some versions of the story, María Luisa was one of the girls who used to visit Gómez.

I take a manila envelope out of my rucksack and look through the photocopied cuttings for a picture of the guy. I find just one, and it's blurry. He's on the way into court, the caption says, for a face-to-face confrontation with two witnesses before the judge. He's an old man in glasses and he's wearing a guayabera shirt.

I remember a conversation I had with a friend in Resistencia, the day I visited the *Norte* newspaper archives to look up articles about the crime, which is where I found that cutting with the photo of Gómez. We went to have fish *milanesas* for lunch, and as we ate we discussed the case. My friend told me that a few years ago he'd been with some fellow activists in a diner not far from the bus terminal. At a nearby table, a guy of around forty was drinking a beer and a girl of twelve was eating a sandwich. They weren't father and daughter. Although my friend didn't catch their conversation, the man's facial expressions, eyes and body language, as he leant in closer and closer over the table, implied that as soon as the little girl finished her ham and cheese roll, their encounter would continue elsewhere. In one of the seedy hotels near the terminal, or right there, in the toilet. The guy was paying in advance, with a lunchtime snack, and afterwards he'd take what he was owed.

I look out of the window. We've left the city now and it's getting dark. We're driving past the zoo. I crane my neck, trying to glimpse the animals, but the trees and bushes around the edge get in the way. All that reaches me is the creaturely smell, carried in the heavy air as the bus crawls along. Fur, feathers, females in heat, baby animals, excrement. And the stagnant water in the troughs and artificial lakes.

I reach Villa Ángela frustrated, tired and sweaty. But it's Saturday. As soon as Monday comes I'll have another go at tracking down Yogui Quevedo. Tonight is the last night of carnival. I'm not a big fan of the *comparsas*, but if you're in Villa Ángela, General San Martín or Quitilipi, attending carnival is more or less compulsory.

It must be some forty degrees centigrade in the moonlight shining down on the corsodrome, a kind of open-air stadium erected along the street outside the old railway station, which is now a cultural centre. The stands have been built on one side of the street. That's where the masses watch from. On the other side there are tables and chairs, where you can enjoy the show a little more comfortably. Since it's the last night of carnival, entrance is free. But the chairs and tables are quite expensive and need to be booked well in advance. I belong to the privileged set who occupy this side of the corsodrome. This year, or this final evening, I'm not sure, there's no table service, unlike other times I've come. Some wooden boards on oil drums, set up in the streets around, become makeshift stalls selling chorizo rolls and beer, which comes in those plastic litre cups big enough to fit the whole bottle. They're not very practical because it takes such balance not to spill half your drink before you reach your table, plus the beer soon gets warm. But it's a sensible measure: carnival night, passions ablaze, a glass in the hand can always end in tragedy.

Some cities in Chaco, and in Corrientes and Entre Ríos, have a long carnival tradition in the style of Rio de Janeiro: huge *comparsas* of scantily-clad dancers, their winged costumes made of feathers – peacock feathers for the most expensive, and dyed ostrich feathers for the rest. Someone at my table says the feathers come from Africa. Their first stop is Brazil, where they're washed and dyed beautiful colours. People once tried making artificial feathers to cut costs, but they were no good. The fake feathers weren't as elegant or supple as the real ones. As well as the feathers, millions of sequins and beads are hand-sewn onto the costumes and boots. A friend of mine makes boots for all the dancers: they're made of tough material, with zips and high heels. Once they leave his little factory, groups of female volunteers (some were dancers in their youth, and others never wanted to be) begin the meticulous embroidery: in the first sweltering siestas of October, sitting in the shade of the trees, drinking *tereré*, they make the first stitches, and then on they go, dazzled by the sun's glare on the sequins, until the end of January.

In Villa Ángela there are two legendary *comparsas*, a third that's slightly newer, and always a fourth that flourishes and dies in that one carnival. The two stalwarts that share the most fans are Ara Sunú – the lower-class one from the wrong side of the tracks, which has the prettiest girls and the finest male bodies, forged by construction and demolition work; and Hawaianas – the fancier one, with the best-groomed girls and gym-toned boys, but also the best samba school. Ara Sunú means stormy weather, or thunder, in Guarani. There's no prize for guessing the meaning of Hawaianas but the name does have one notable feature, which is that the locals pronounce it *aguaiana*, overly respecting the silent H at the beginning and skipping the final S. As with football, the people of Villa Ángela are supporters, or fans, of one or the other.

This evening I'm at a table of Hawaianas devotees, though secretly my heart belongs to Ara Sunú.

The third group in the parade was once controversial, because it arose from a fight between the couple who ran Ara Sunú: they split up, and when they shared out their possessions he took a few loyal followers and founded this group, Bahía, which is now a respectable size. And this year's flash in the pan is Samberos de Itá Verá, who will come last in the parade, paying their dues as the newbies.

Unlike in the Rio *comparsas*, there isn't a single transvestite. In this city of people descended from the first immigrants to populate the country, and others who followed later from Eastern Europe, people are conservative. Neither transvestites nor homosexuals of any kind are welcome around here. Still, it's inevitable that some gay people slip into the hallowed ranks of carnival and live those four wild nights to the fullest, stamping their heels on the corsodrome's concrete floor, crotches thrust out, shiny microscopic G-strings shaking to the rhythm of the drums.

The first *comparsa*, Ara Sunú, goes by, and when they announce the second I decide it's a good time to go to the bathroom: in the intervals it's impossible.

Even now, there's a queue outside the first two portable toilets I come to. They aren't divided into women's and men's, but the queues form according to the gender of the people waiting. In front of me, two girls of ten or eleven, and another of five. Outside the next cubicle, six guys. This part of the street is dark and the toilets are right by a building site. The girls, on the cusp of adolescence, dressed in hot pants and vests that press tight against their budding nipples, practise dance moves on the spot, twirling their wrists like the older girls who strut their stuff in the corsodrome. They critique their attempts at a particular step, one explains to the other how to do it properly. Some of the guys queuing for the toilet watch.

I don't like them looking at the girls, although in the gloom I can't tell how they're looking at them. When the youngest comes out, rearranging her pink shorts, another of the girls says I can go next. Although I'm about to wet myself, I smile and say no, they can go, I'll keep an eye on the door. And I raise my voice for the last part, so our neighbours at the other toilet can hear me. Just in case.

The rest of the night will follow the same pattern: the *comparsa* goes by with some two hundred and something members, a spray-foam fight in the interval, trips to the bathroom and refreshment stands, and so on until the early hours.

When we're finally heading towards the cars parked in a field nearby, I hear a still-childish voice shouting: As if I'd let you fuck me, are you crazy, you fucking fag, you piece of shit. A girl of around twelve who looks like one of my friends from the toilet queue, dark-skinned, thin, followed by a gaggle of kids of a similar age, is having a slanging match with a cluster of guys. Although her opponents have now fallen silent and are backing away, embarrassed by the girl's filthy mouth, she follows them in order to keep yelling.

A feisty little carnival kid. A girl alone on a carnival night.

After Sunday lunch one day, Coco Valdez, my father-in-law, tells me about the time he saw a dead girl. They were having dinner one night with his wife's parents, who had a little café opposite the train station. Someone knocked at the door and he went to see who it was. A boy he knew, whose surname was Lencina, asked if he could use their phone to call the police. Yes, of course, come inside, but what was going on? On some waste ground, not far away, Lencina had come across the body of a

62

woman. He couldn't be sure because it was night-time, although the moon was bright, but he thought she was dead and he didn't want to touch her.

They waited in the café, which was closed at that hour, for the police to arrive. The officer came on a bicycle because the patrol car was at the garage being repaired.

Have you got a vehicle? he asked Coco. Come on, come with us.

Lencina led them through the wasteland. In the weeds, by the side of a path that had formed by being used as a shortcut, they found the girl. When the police officer shone a torch on her face, the three of them looked at one another, stunned. She was a Carahuni, the daughter of a traditional family in the town, and related to Coco Carahuni, a well-known car dealer. Someone had stabbed her in the stomach.

My father-in-law drove away in his truck with the girl's corpse, the police officer and Lencina, who had quickly turned from a witness to a suspect, though they released him the next day. The boy had nothing to do with it, he'd just had the bad luck to be crossing the wasteland.

The Carahuni crime remains a mystery, forty years on. At the time, a man from Rosario who'd recently moved to Villa Ángela was arrested for the girl's murder, but they never found a motive. Apparently the man had threatened his wife: If you don't stop messing me around, I'll deal with you like I dealt with that Carahuni girl. And she reported him to the police.

Someone else around the table recalls a more recent case, from 1997, involving Andrea Strumberger, a girl of sixteen and a secondary school student. She was an Evangelical Christian and that Sunday she set off on her moped for the Asamblea de Dios Evangelical church.

She never arrived, and the next day her body showed up in some wasteland. She'd been raped and beaten to death. Her brother-in-law was arrested for the murder. Everyone knew him, because he was the relative who'd called the most vocally for the case to be resolved.

On Monday I go back to Sáenz Peña. Uninvited, without calling ahead, without agreeing a time or place. I get there in the morning. I'm going to find Yogui Quevedo whatever it takes, and we're going to talk.

Not that it will be easy. The helpful man I spoke to on the phone a few months ago has suddenly turned evasive.

I call his mobile as soon as I arrive. No luck despite several attempts, always the voicemail.

It's mid-morning and I'm in the city centre. Last time I was here I saw it from a bus, then a taxi, then I walked a few blocks. Today I have more time, and since Yogui isn't picking up, I set off down the pedestrianised street in search of a bar. The heat is stifling and a cold drink somewhere with air con would be good. Wait in the shade.

The pedestrianised Calle San Martín must be about ten blocks long, and I walk all the way down it looking in shop windows. There are no bars. On my whole expedition I find just one. I look in from outside and see several tables with people at them, all men of fifty or more, drinking whisky or beer, smoking and talking in loud voices. Surely I passed more than one bar, I think, and I walk up and down the street again. But no, it seems the bar full of shouting men is the only one. I ask in a kiosk: where can I find a bar that'll do me a soft drink, somewhere quiet. They point to an ice-cream parlour. I don't want an ice cream, I want a cold drink. Yep, you can get that there too. I head towards it with misgivings, thinking they've seen I'm not from around there and are playing a joke on me. But no, the bar I was looking for is an ice-cream parlour. Later I learn that in Sáenz Peña there are almost no bars. The teenagers and young people don't normally go to bars to drink. Instead they park their cars, motorbikes and pickups outside the kiosks and drink on the pavement until it's time to go to the nightclub.

I order a Sprite in the ice-cream parlour and they bring me a litre bottle, they don't sell anything smaller. It's almost like a premonition, because I'm in for a long wait. After more failed attempts, someone finally answers Yogui's phone. It's not him; another man says that yes, this is Quevedo's number, but he can't talk because he's in a meeting and I should call back at midday.

I take a book someone lent me out of my rucksack. It's called *Twenty-five Murders from the Sáenz Peña Crime Pages*, by the local historian Raúl López. One story catches my eye, the one about the Polish girl and the Paraguayan guy, which took place in the fifties.

Rosa was the daughter of a Polish couple. She was a sportswoman and worked in a shop, La Ideal, one of those big stores that sell everything: clothes, shoes, wedding dresses, cuts of fabric, bed linen and towels, catering for all the family. As captain of the women's volleyball team, she'd won a handful of medals and trophies in provincial and national games. The photo accompanying the article shows her on a trip with her teammates: she was a beautiful girl, robust and healthy. In the same club where she achieved this sporting success, she met the person who would be first her lover and then her murderer: Juan, a young Paraguayan who'd got a job in the sports club bar. The attraction was immediate: she a little cautious, shy; he overpowering, persistent, sticky like the scent of the orange blossom that scatters the streets of his country. They began dating. Her parents didn't approve of the relationship, but she was ready for anything, she'd never been so in love, never had anyone whisper such tender words in her ear, never felt so womanly or so desired as she did on that cheap hotel bed where she made love with Juan whenever she could sneak out of the house.

However, her boyfriend soon showed himself for what he was: a possessive, jealous and violent man. Rosa, even head over heels in love, was a woman of character. The ladies' volleyball captain got the better of the dreamy girlfriend and she broke off the relationship. Needless to say, Juan didn't take it calmly. After the entreaties and passionate declarations came threats. And a letter printed in the town paper describing every last detail of his relations with the girl. An equivalent to the videos posted online by malicious ex-lovers more than fifty years later: the public exposure of a woman's privacy. Rosa must have thought he couldn't go any further, that nothing could be worse for a decent, hard-working girl like her than to be stripped naked and shamed by that letter. She must have thought that if she'd survived public humiliation at the hand of her ex-boyfriend, he had no weapons left that could crush her. She got used to looking over her shoulder: no matter where she went, sooner or later she'd see him. Rejected, he'd turned to drink and lost his job. So not only did he follow her around, but when they crossed paths he yelled abuse at her, the wine slurring his words, which were always offensive.

As a precaution, she tried not to go out alone. Her mother went with her to work every day, and met her outside when she finished. One morning, the two of them were walking along arm in arm. They saw him on a street corner, but that wasn't unusual and they carried on past, brisk, indifferent, heads high. So set on ignoring him that the hand must have come as a surprise, clasping her shoulder from behind and pulling her around, and Juan's bloodshot eyes that seemed to beg her one last time, then the same hand drawing her towards him and the other sliding a knife into her flesh, and then her tumbling, both of them tumbling to the pavement as he stabbed her again and again, and her mother screaming, running for help. Rosa staring at him, still not understanding. Taking a long time to die. Him on top of her, thrusting the knife in and out. Her beneath him, just like in the cheap hotel bed. Him splattered all over with blood. Then, unable to bear Rosa's blue-eyed gaze, Juan slit her throat from side to side, before plunging the same knife into his own stomach. The two bodies in a heap, spilling blood onto the pavement, just outside the shop.

Earlier, walking around, I passed the House of Culture, a large old building that had been renovated. A plaque said it used to be the Ideal store. I leave the ice-cream parlour and wander towards it. Somewhere on that block, Rosa was killed.

It's noon on the dot and I call Yogui again. Finally he's the one who picks up. I tell him I'm in the city, that I've come to interview him. That I came on Saturday as we agreed but couldn't get hold of him, that he never answered my messages or calls. He says he was at a function with the governor all afternoon. That we can meet in half an hour at his brothers' travel agency.

I'm a few blocks away, no more than five minutes, so I cross into the main square and sit on a bench to wait for the time to pass.

When half an hour's almost up and I'm making my way over, I see two men chatting on the pavement. One must be Yogui, I think, without deciding which. Based on their ages it could be either. I say hello and introduce myself, and then one of them, short and dark-skinned, with large, almond-shaped eyes like a deer's, holds out his hand. I thought you'd be older, he says, with a winning smile. He explains to the other man, who also shakes my hand, that I'm from Buenos Aires and I'm going to write a book about his sister. The man nods and says goodbye. Yogui invites me to sit on the same low wall where I sat last time. I feel the warm concrete through the fabric of my jeans. He tells me he's waiting for the minibus from Bolivia, that his brothers are on their way back from a trip. I tell him I know, I spoke to one of them on the phone, that when I couldn't get hold of him as arranged I called the mobile number on the board outside. He looks at me solemnly and asks if I told his brother what it was about. I say yes. He shakes his head. No, no, he says, they don't want anything to do with this, I'm the only one who keeps going with it all. He says we should meet later instead, they won't like seeing me with him when they arrive, and besides, he has to work. He works with them, he emphasises, as if my being there put his source of employment at risk.

Here at five, ok? I'm by myself in the evenings.

He's just finished speaking when the white minibus pulls in, packed with people and equipment. The driver gets out, waves at his brother and glances at me, then carries on walking towards the office. Yogui doesn't introduce us.

See you later, he says, I can't talk now. And he shakes my hand again.

I check the time on my phone. It's almost five hours until five o'clock. I walk all the way down the pedestrianised street again, this time looking for a restaurant. There aren't many options. I go for one at the end nearest the square, because I know that's where I'll have to spend all the remaining hours until five.

I order a sandwich and a mineral water. I watch the news on TV, and every time I reach for my glass I have to peel my arm off the rubber seat. There aren't many customers. My gaze shifts from the TV to the window, which will be busier than the screen until a quarter past one. From then on, deserted, motionless. The city has stopped and it won't start again until five.

I sit on a bench in the shade and take off my trainers. I rub the soles of my feet on the rough, close-cropped grass. It's very hot. Not the slightest breeze. The only souls out and about at this hour are a man in his fifties with very dark hair and a bag in his hand, a tradesman dozing on the ground with his head resting on his rucksack, two kissing teenagers half-hidden by a tree, and me. No people, no cars, no dogs. All shut up safe and sound in their houses, waiting for the fierce heat to subside. If I listen closely, I think I can catch the soft humming of the split air con units, the motorised clanking of the older systems, the patter of ceiling fans. I'm jealous. I should have found a hotel, if only for the siesta.

Before me stands the cathedral, magnanimous. The further a place from the hand of God, the more imposing the building that honours him. On the day María Luisa went missing, the cathedral and the square would have been teeming with the faithful, worshipping the Immaculate Conception. Maybe she even passed this way, unnoticed in the crowd, to leave a flower for the Virgin. From my place in the square, I can see that it's closed. Pity. I would have liked to go in: it's always cooler inside churches.

I decide not to look at the time again. Whenever I take out my phone and check, only a few minutes have gone by. I set the alarm for five to five.

Suddenly I see them appear in a corner of the square. I don't know if they're real or part of a dream. From a distance the figures look hazy, their outlines rippling like a mirage. When they get closer, I see that they're real. Two Mennonite men in denim dungarees, check shirts with the sleeves rolled up to the elbows, black lace-up shoes, white hats, and bags in their hands. Behind them, emerging into view as they draw nearer, two women in flowery dresses and aprons, with blue scarves covering their hair. One has a baby in her arms. Not far from the city there's a Mennonite community. Their bags must be full of the cheeses and homemade produce they make and bring here to sell.

They cross the road, seeking the shade on the pavement. I watch as they drift slowly along, more prisoners of the siesta. They stop at the huge window of a home appliances store and gaze in as if sharing something illicit, a minor sin: feasting their eyes for a time on those forbidden inventions.

I follow the tradesman's lead and stretch out on the bench, my rucksack under my head. I must have fallen asleep at some point because I wake up in the middle of a dream in which thousands of cicadas are singing in unison. It's my phone alarm vibrating inside my rucksack. Five to five.

I sit up and pull on my trainers. Gradually things begin to stir. The street fills up with mopeds. The odd car, the odd bicycle, people on foot. The shops open at five.

I stop in a service station and ask for the key to the toilet. I wash my face, neaten up my hair, put some chewing gum in my mouth. I can feel my heart beating faster. Finally I'm going to talk to María Luisa's brother.

But not at five, as we'd agreed. Yogui Quevedo keeps me waiting another half-hour, sitting yet again on that blessed wall.

As I wait, I have the feeling I'm being watched. I look up at the big broken windows of the building, which has another two floors above the Quevedos' office. I think I see a curtain move. I feel slightly uneasy. I type out a message and press send. Yogui replies that he's on his way. All in capitals, as if he's shouting, as if we were still too far apart for me to hear him. And we must be, since it's another fifteen minutes before he shows up.

Finally I see him come round the corner and cross the street, smiling at me. He holds out his hand. He's just showered, his shiny black hair is flat against his skull, and he smells of an aftershave that reminds me of one my father used to use. He doesn't apologise for being late.

He takes out a key and opens the door. We step into a dim, down-at-heel little office. He puts the envelope he's been holding on the rickety Formica table that serves as a desk and tells me to make myself at home. I sit on one of the three chairs, which are also made of Formica. He puts a fan near the open door. I look over. There's a large carob-wood shelving unit opposite chock full of spirits and whisky bottles, lined up and covered in dirt. They must buy them on those trips they make to the border, meaning to sell them on, and then they accumulate there, forgotten. As well as that table there's another, smaller one, at the back, with a portable stove on top connected to a gas cylinder. He lights it and starts heating some water. While he prepares the *mate*, we talk about the weather. They said on the radio that it's going to rain this evening, but the sky is blue and cloudless.

He comes over to the table with the *mate* ready and sits down. He slides the envelope towards me.

I brought you something.

I look at him, I look at the envelope, but I don't move.

It's a photo of my sister.

I've still never seen a photo of María Luisa. Just a pencil sketch in the paper. I'm interested to know what she really looked like. The drawing I saw was very rough, like one of those identikits the police put together. But my hands don't do as I tell them and I go on staring at the envelope without opening it, without even touching it.

It's a photo of her in the morgue, he says eventually.

My stomach turns over.

I don't know if you'll want to see it. I bought it off a police photographer.

I can't understand why anyone would want to have a photo like that. Before I have the chance to ask, he tells me: Since here they did fuck all, I got in touch with a magazine in Buenos Aires, one of the true crime ones. *Esto*, I think it was. Anyway, you know how those magazines like morbid shit. And I wanted the rest of the country to know about my sister's murder, in case that gave people here a kick up the arse.

I'm not convinced by his explanation, but I reach for the envelope and quickly pull out the photo. It's an enlargement. I glance at it briefly. The poor thing. I check inside the envelope, hoping he's also brought one of María Luisa alive. But there's nothing else. I look up and he's watching me.

See how she ended up. Completely disfigured. I only recognised her because of a scar on her leg, from when I chucked a tape player at her one time.

You threw a tape player at her?

Yeah, we were arguing. You know what brothers and sisters are like. I didn't mean to actually hurt her...

I'd like to see a photo of her.

I don't have any. There was one in the paper, of her with my mum and my sister-in-law, but it got lost.

The fan by the door just drags the hot air in from outside and moves it in circles above us. I'm sweating, and I feel a bit annoyed and also a bit tired. Or sad.

I tell him the *mate*'s got cold. Maybe if we go back to the moment when we'd just arrived, if he puts the kettle on the stove again and adds fresh leaves and comes back and sits down and I forget about the envelope with the photo, we can start the interview.

He waits for the kettle to start whistling and sprinkles more *mate* leaves into the gourd. He drinks the first one, then refills it and passes it to me.

Better?

I nod, and tell him I'm surprised he doesn't drink *tereré* like everyone else there.

We've got no fridge.

Has he been working with his brothers for long?

On and off, helping them out. I took voluntary retirement. For a long time I worked driving a rubbish truck.

I ask if he remembers the last time he saw his sister and he tells me it was the same day she disappeared, around 10 a.m. He was on a bus, on his way to the job he had then in a radio repair shop, and since it was a holiday or half-holiday he was going in later than usual. He saw her through the window: she was on the pavement outside the house where she worked as a maid, she had a shopping bag in her hand and was talking to a boy on a bicycle, leaning on the handlebars as they chatted. The boy was Francisco Suárez, an employee of Don Gómez, who Yogui knew by sight. Were it not for what happened afterwards, he'd probably have forgotten the scene: his teenage sister flirting with a boy on the pavement. If things had carried on as normal, perhaps

73

he'd only have remembered in order to tease her, the way older brothers do when their sisters are discovering boys.

Did she have a boyfriend? Was this Suárez guy her boyfriend?

No, no. Well, not that I know of...

Yogui was twelve years older than María Luisa, so yes, he probably wouldn't have known.

He tells me María Luisa didn't go to school and her only friends were from the neighbourhood. She was a real homebody, and this was her first job.

However, in that short, intense week that marked her leaving the house to join the adult world, the world of going out to work, María Luisa made two friends: Norma Romero and Elena Taborda, two girls slightly older than her, and more streetwise. Quevedo blames them for leading her astray. As if her death were a punishment for something she'd been doing wrong. According to him, that day, probably the last of María Luisa's short life, she met up with her new friends after work and they invited her to spend the afternoon in Villa Bermejito, a village around sixty miles away on the banks of a tributary of the Bermejo river, where people had weekend homes. They were going with Francisco Suárez, Catalino Lencina and Jesús Gómez, the boss of the first two.

That's what the girls said the first time they were questioned, and their statement was backed up by a petrol station attendant who confirmed that he'd filled up a car containing Don Gómez, two guys and three girls. But Norma and Elena, when called before the judge, denied everything they'd told the police and filed a complaint of unlawful coercion, showing the marks from beatings they'd received to make them give false testimony.

The judge for the case, Oscar Sudría, believes the two girls hold the key. He's convinced that they (and the murderer or murderers) are the only people left who can say exactly what happened on that December 8th.

Over the twenty years it took him to close the case, he summoned them several times to make statements. It wasn't easy because the girls left Sáenz Peña soon after the murder and never stayed long in the same place. So every two or three years, first he had to find out where they were, and then he had to bring them back. He saw them at weekends, never with the police, because, after their complaints of illegal coercion during the 1983 investigation, if there was anyone they didn't trust it was the police. As the years went by, he watched them grow into women, have children. But he could never get a word out of either of them.

The petrol station attendant, when called in to make another statement, changed his story as well: he'd never seen Don Gómez and María Luisa together.

Quevedo maintains that they're lying, that these key witnesses in his sister's rape and murder were bought off by Gómez and his immense fortune – Gómez, who even Quevedo still calls Don Gómez, as if he inspired in him a strange sort of fear or respect.

We're interrupted by his phone. He answers and begins a conversation, practically shouting. The signal's bad, it's a call from Buenos Aires.

On the other end is an adviser to the Chaco politician Antonio Morante. They chat for a bit. Quevedo tells him about me, hands me the phone, the adviser and I say hello, he tells me something about a bill they're putting forward in the Chamber, we swap email addresses. I return the handset, Yogui says a few more words then hangs up. He seems pleased. Since the line wasn't great, I didn't fully understand about the bill they're planning to present in the Honourable Chamber of Deputies of the Nation.

I go several times to see the Señora. The green cloth folded in half, which was on the coffee table that first afternoon, is always there. She keeps the pack of tarot cards inside it. Each time, she peels the cloth back carefully, as if uncovering a sleeping child. She asks me to cut the deck into three. Then to shuffle each third, moving the cards in a circle, seven times, with my right hand. She forms a stack again and we hold hands over the freshly shuffled deck, saying aloud the name and surname of the girl we want to ask about. Then she draws cards and lays them on the cloth one by one. I see the figures upside-down. It makes no difference because I don't know what they mean.

Other times, the girls get in ahead of the cards.

One afternoon she says she can't breathe and raises a hand to her throat. She stays like that, her eyes closed. I sit still. All I can do is wait until whatever's happening to her stops happening. When she comes to, opens her mouth and takes a breath, her eyes are shining.

I couldn't breathe, I was suffocating, it was so intense. Pressure here and a pain here, she says, pointing first to her neck and then between her legs.

It's María Luisa, strangled and raped.

Poor little thing. Pulled up like a reed. She was still so young, with so weak a hold on life. Like the reeds that grow beside lakes, she says to me.

I remember the photos I saw of María Luisa. The one her brother showed me of her body in the morgue, swollen,

81

muddy, with parts of her face eaten by birds. And another two I saw in the case file.

One is also of her body, in the place where they found her. It's taken from a short distance away, and it's in black and white. It shows the body of a woman floating in the water. This photo reminds me of the painting by John Millais, of the dead Ophelia. Like the character from *Hamlet*, María Luisa is floating face-up. Like in the painting, the flat green reeds curve over the lake, and the surface is covered in tiny aquatic plants. Not the purple flowers Queen Gertrude calls dead men's fingers, and that Ophelia wove into her crowns, but others, known as duckweed. A tree, not the willow young Ophelia falls from, but one with a low, squat canopy, casts its shadow over María Luisa's body. Death, for both of them, shot through with anguish.

The other photo is in colour and in it María Luisa is alive. It's a family photo, of a group of women. Maybe it was taken on someone's birthday. On the left is her little sister, then her mother in a fancy housecoat, then one of her sisters-in-law holding a baby girl, and finally María Luisa. All the others, even the baby, are smiling at the camera. But not her. She's wearing a white vest that stands out against her brown skin, and she's not smiling. Under her thick fringe, her large, serious eyes look slightly downwards and off to one side. She seems sad.

No one forced María Luisa. She went on that trip, or whatever it was, because she wanted to. Maybe she was invited by the boy her brother saw her with, maybe they were going out or she was in love with him, or maybe her friends convinced her. But it wasn't a kidnapping. She wanted to go. Then, for some reason, it all went to pieces. She's not annoyed. I don't think she understands what happened, even now. She was still so young. For her, everything was new: the new job, the new friends, that boy...

I think we have to find a way of reconstructing how the world saw them. If we can understand how people saw the girls, we'll be able to understand how they saw the world, does that make sense?

Teenagers or even children having jobs was common in towns in the interior, at least until the eighties. You didn't have to be from a particularly poor family. Girls from working-class homes, whose mothers did the housework, were sent out to work by these same mothers from when they were very young.

My best friend in those days had a job as a babysitter from the age of ten, when she was barely older than the kids she looked after. My mum had also worked from when she was young, and because of that we weren't allowed to. Strangely, I felt a bit jealous of my friend's situation: she earned a wage, not much of one but a wage all the same, which meant she had money of her own; she had responsibilities, she spent a lot of each day out of her house, and what's more, she went to school and got good grades, like me. In my eyes my friend was superior. Confident, streetwise.

And yet my other friends didn't see her that way. To them, my friend was beneath us: she had to work and we didn't. Even though the most those girls could aspire to was qualifying as teachers and marrying kind, hard-working men.

Andrea didn't have to work as a girl either. The only person in her house who worked was her father. In a meat processing plant. She was able to study because her boyfriend paid for it. If he hadn't come along, maybe Andrea would have ended up working in the Vizental like most young people in San José, who finished secondary school, if that, then put their names down, took a seat and waited to be called. Plant worker or secretary. Andrea, being pretty, would have got a job in the admin department. Well-dressed, well-groomed and always sweet-smelling, even in the fetid black cloud of boiled meat, the secretaries typed on typewriters and did sums on calculators and strode down the corridors with their arms full of files and their feet falling neatly in line, that elegant gait. Ogled by the workers, who, as they sawed up hooves, tails and heads, and separated skin from flesh, felt as frisky as bulls and dreamed of mounting the secretaries like cows.

If the possibility ever crossed her mind, it can't have been very appealing. The memory of her father coming back from the slaughterhouse every afternoon, smelling of blood and disinfectant, must have turned her stomach.

Sarita also started work young. She had no choice, because in her family they were very poor. The last job she had before getting married was as a cleaner in a doctor's house. They treated her well there, almost like a daughter, and encouraged her to study. But she fell pregnant and got married. She was too pretty for her husband to send out as a maid again, all that beauty going to waste in a haze of cleaning products. So he sent her out as a prostitute.

Andrea wanted something different, the Señora says. It's not true that she dreamed of getting married, having children and qualifying as a teacher. If Andrea hadn't been killed, she would have upped sticks. She wanted out. She didn't see any future where she was.

In the tarot cards a lover appears, an older man. In the case file, too.

I knew him. He lived a few blocks from my house at the time of the murder. But I knew him from before. He was called Pepe Durand and he was a driver with the El Directo bus company, which made short trips from my town to nearby towns and cities. Sometimes, when I went to visit my grandparents in the countryside, I'd take the bus there with my aunts and he'd be driving. He was a good-looking guy. At least, my aunts liked him, especially the youngest, who'd deposit me in a seat with the bags then go off and spend the whole journey chatting to him. Standing behind his seat as they talked, leaning on the backrest and laughing loudly, a high-pitched laugh like a whinnying colt. Sometimes she also prepared *mate* and passed him the gourd. I don't know if anything ever happened between them, but I'm sure my aunt had a crush on Pepe.

Despite being so popular with women – sometimes I took the bus alone or with my parents, and without my aunts, and I'd always see another girl standing behind the driver's seat, also shrieking with laughter – Pepe was a man of few words, and not very sociable.

People said he was odd, with that inflection they put on the word when they meant a person wasn't quite right. Sometimes he went to the *boliche*, a bar called El Ombú. *Boliches* were the meeting places for lower-middle-class men who couldn't go and get drunk in the Jockey Club like professionals and the children of respectable families. According to the Ombú regulars, when Pepe went to the bar he never sat with anyone, he just drank alone while watching whatever game was showing on TV. He didn't get involved in the talk about politics, football or women. If they ever tried to include him, he nodded from where he was sitting, without opening his mouth. An odd guy.

Not quite right.

When he moved into a house near us, he brought a younger woman with him – he'd have been around forty at the time. No one knew anything about her, because she was from out of town and kept herself to herself. The mystery couple were the talk of the neighbourhood. And when he was linked to Andrea's murder, the whispers multiplied like flies around a carcass.

Pepe drove the bus that took students from Villa Elisa, Colón and San José to Concepción del Uruguay, for the teacher training programmes and other vocational courses taught in that city. Andrea was one of the students who travelled with El Directo every day.

In the case file, some people who used to take the same bus said the driver and the girl were romantically involved; that when everyone else got out at the terminal, she stayed on the bus with him, and that sometimes they saw the pair having dinner by themselves in a little reataurant nearby. The owner of a boarding house by the terminal also said she rented him a room, which she'd seen him going into with the murdered girl. And a girl who studied with Andrea said he'd shown up at the teacher training college one evening that year. They were in class and he called to her from the courtyard. Andrea went out and they spoke for a bit, and when she came back in, the girl asked if her father had come to find her because something had happened at home. Andrea said it was nothing, and that he was a friend, not her father.

When summoned to give a statement, he denied all involvement with her beyond the bus journeys. He knew her by sight, as he did most of the students he took there and back, maybe they'd chatted once or twice or she'd borrowed the kit to make herself some *mate*. But that was it. The night of the murder, he said, he'd gone for a walk with his wife. Since it was so hot, they spent a long time sitting in the square, then headed home because a storm was brewing. His wife never contradicted him.

Still, it was a long time before the police left him alone. In the months that followed, I often saw patrol cars driving slowly around the dirt roads of my neighbourhood. We all knew who they were watching.

He didn't kill Andrea. He was in love with her, says the Señora. In some ancient cultures, it was thought that the soul lived in the eyes, you know? And so lovers swapped souls by looking at each other: I'd give you mine, and you'd give me yours. But when one person stopped loving the other, they'd get their soul back and keep their lover's soul as well. When one of them dies, it must be the same. Andrea took Pepe's soul with her.

He said he heard about Andrea's death the same way most people did, on the radio that day, on the 7 a.m. departure from Villa Elisa to Concepción del Uruguay. It must be awful to learn of the death of a loved one like that, to have to keep driving the bus as if the news, the worst you could ever receive, were just another of the countless daily misfortunes that always happen to other people.

One morning a couple of years ago, Pepe was found dead. He hanged himself from a roof beam in his house.

Andrea's mother was called Gloria and she was suspected, along with her husband, of murdering the girl. In her statement, she said she found her daughter's body after a noise woke her up, a scream or a premonition, she was never sure which. She'd shut the bedroom window overlooking the yard herself, not long before going back and finding her daughter had been stabbed. The kitchen door was closed as well. It was a small house, with just three rooms, all interconnected by doors.

Blood was found on her clothes, of the same blood group as Andrea's, though she claimed never to have touched the body. Not in an attempt to revive her, and not for a final embrace when they were certain she was dead. The blood on her clothes, she said, may have come from her husband, whose shirt did have blood on it because he'd come into contact with the corpse. The couple had hugged each other, for consolation.

Those who knew her remember her as a withdrawn woman, odd and rather distant. At the time of the murder, Gloria was forty-six, the age Andrea would be now. She was a housewife.

After finding the girl in bed covered in blood, the father and a neighbour went to get the family doctor, Raúl Favre. When the doctor came into the bedroom, Gloria was sitting on the other bed, hands clasped in her lap, staring into space. Like an autistic person, he said. And according to close witnesses, she remained like that for the rest of the morning, and in the funeral chapel when the body was returned to them, and in the weeks that followed her daughter's death. As if she'd been anaesthetised.

Back then I remember people saying Gloria went to get her hair done the day after the murder. Everyone was horrified at the thought: a woman who'd just experienced the worst thing imaginable for a mother, taking a seat in the hairdresser's chair. That act, which could also have been a way of distracting herself from the nightmare she was living, was immediately taken as a sign of guilt.

It seems we expect a mother with a dead daughter to tear out her hair, to weep inconsolably, to shake her fist and beg for revenge. We don't tolerate calm. We don't forgive resignation.

Last year Ángeles Rawson, a girl of sixteen, was killed in the Colegiales neighbourhood, in Buenos Aires. Ángeles was missing for almost twenty-four hours and then her body was found on the conveyor belt at a waste processing plant, some miles from the capital. When she learnt what had happened, Ángeles' mum said: No human being is less important than the worst thing they have ever done, and she was harshly criticised for these words. We don't accept mothers being pious, either.

As well as being accused of murdering her daughter, or at least of participating in the murder and cover-up, and of going to the hairdresser, Gloria is blamed for not attending any of the marches demanding justice for Andrea, not attending a single mass held in her memory, not lifting a finger to help resolve the case, and repeating, whenever she was called in for questioning, the same story, right down to every full stop and comma, as if she were following a script.

She outlived her daughter by twenty-four years. Curiously, they both died on the same day: November 16th.

Andrea's father always comes out on the side of the violence, the Señora tells me, laying the cards on the table again and again. Are you sure he was her real father?

I thought so at the time. But later I learnt of a rumour that Gloria had been seeing a boy from the countryside who died in a motorbike crash. When she realised she was pregnant, she married another suitor, Eymar Danne, who, whether or not he knew about what happened, ended up becoming Andrea's dad.

There's no proof of this, but if it's true, I think, what a destiny: father and daughter both violently killed at such a young age.

Eymar Danne worked in a meat plant and in his free time he liked to make knives. There were knives he'd made all over the house. Lots of knives. But after the night of the murder, one was missing. Maybe the one that was used to stab Andrea.

María Luisa's mother also died several years ago. The only one who's still alive is Sara Páez de Mundín, the mother of Sarita. She still lives in the city of Villa María in Córdoba province, in a poor neighbourhood on the outskirts. I go and see her one winter Sunday. It's cold and overcast. There's no one in the streets, no children playing football or dogs to come snapping at the wheels of the taxi when we drive by. A restless wind lifts the loose dirt in the street into eddies.

The taxi driver drops me at a house with nothing growing outside. The bare earth reaches all the way from the street to the front door. Sara lets me in. She's one of those women whose age is difficult to work out. She has short, curly hair, dark with some grey. A face carved with wrinkles. A mannish air. You can tell she's a woman who's suffered, who life and bad luck have never given a break.

We go into a room containing nothing but a gas cooker. It's nice and warm because she has the oven on. There's a smell of empanadas cooking. She tells me she makes them to order, to earn money so she can travel to the city of Córdoba, where her husband is in hospital. We go through to the other room, where there's a table with three chairs, a dresser and a double bed. I sit at the table and Sara opts for the end of her bed.

She arrived in Villa María in the early hours of this morning, and this evening she's going back to the hospital in Córdoba to look after her husband, who seems to be in a very bad way. Her health isn't so good either.

A few months before Sarita's disappearance, Sara lost another child. She said another child of hers was killed, although really the boy died playing football – he had a heart attack. She says they made him play, that he knew he couldn't because of his health problems, and that's why he didn't just die but was killed. And a few months after Sarita, she lost a granddaughter, the girl her other daughter, Mirta, was expecting.

I'll go and get Mirta, she lives just round the back, she says, and leaves the room.

I'm left alone. The grimy daylight filters in through a small window. A yellow bulb hanging from the ceiling lights the room. There's not much to see on the bare walls, no paintings or anything. That's why the photo is so noticeable, at the head of the bed, where other people hang a crucifix. I move closer. It must be Sarita. She has a short, eighties hairdo, red plastic hoop earrings and a black pullover with fuchsia swirls. Quietly beautiful, she looks at the camera with a slight smile.

I'm still looking at the photo when I hear the voice of Sara, now back.

That was my daughter, and this is my other daughter, Mirta.

We say hello. Mirta is also a good-looking woman, but with a harder, wilder beauty, her hair long and jet-black, her eyes large and dark.

They both sit down, once again on the end of the bed.

Sarita was a very good daughter, she was always helping me out. If she saw my trainers were falling apart, she wouldn't say anything, she'd just go to the shop and get me another pair. She always made sure I had everything I needed. And when I came out of hospital, a few days before she disappeared, she took me to the apartment where she lived with the boy and Mirta, to look after me until I could take care of myself.

Sara doesn't remember much about the last day they saw Sarita. She'd just had an operation and was taking a lot of tranquillisers for the pain, so she was feeling a bit woozy. She remembers being in bed and her daughter coming to say goodbye, with a towel in her hand. And Marta saying the next day that Sarita hadn't come back, and feeling worried, but not being able to get up to look for her, and Mirta and some friends going to report her disappearance to the police. A few weeks later, when she still hadn't come back, they had to leave the little apartment that Dady Olivero, her daughter's lover, paid for on Sarita's behalf.

Since he was the last person she was seen with, Mirta called him before anyone else to ask what he'd done with her sister. He said that after going for a drive in his car, he'd dropped her near the bus terminal. They asked at all the ticket windows, and tried all the porters and taxi drivers, but nobody had seen her.

Nine months later, at the end of December 1988, a woman's remains showed up on the banks of the Tcalamochita river. Mirta went to the morgue to identify them.

They told me those bones were Sarita's. A load of white bones. They picked one up and showed it to me. Look: long bones, from a tall woman. They took a skull out of a box, with a few hairs stuck to the crown. They opened the jaw and showed me the teeth with fillings. Sarita had had some things done to her teeth, but what do I know, it could have been her but it could have been someone else. All it looked like to me was a pile of bones.

In the case file, the discovery is described as follows:

The skeleton was found at the tip of the island, at the place called La Herradura, in a tangle of debris left by the flooding of the Tcalamochita river, comprising a fallen tree into which branches and logs had been enmeshed, in addition to rubbish borne along by the water (bottles, polystyrene). The remains were found lying perpendicular to the course of the river, in a supine position, with the legs facing towards the bank; the right side against the current and the left flank protected from the same. The skeleton presented more damage on the right side than on the left, and the top of the skull more than the lower part. Women's clothing was present: knickers, brassiere, skirt and the remains of a polo shirt.

The remains of the clothing they showed me were just scraps of rotting rags, Mirta recalls, so I couldn't say if it was what Sarita was wearing that afternoon or not. They also found a necklace nearby that looked like one my sister used to have. In the end, a dentist who said he'd treated her identified the body by the teeth.

Sara never believed the skeleton belonged to her daughter. She always thought Dady Olivero was behind Sarita's disappearance. When those remains were found, Olivero went to prison for a few months. Contradicting Mirta, he said he hadn't seen Sarita the day she disappeared, he hadn't taken her for any kind of outing, his relationship with the girl had ended a few months before and she'd once said to him: Baby, I'm mixed up in so much shit that sometimes I just want to get the hell out. He said that between March and April of that year, he'd been with relatives in the city of Salta, where his wife had family. He was planning to open some butchers' shops there and went to set things up. Olivero's wife confirmed his alibi.

Since it was never possible to say how Sarita died, the only person suspected of her disappearance was ultimately released.

Ten years later, Sara found out about a new test that could identify human remains, even if they were just bones: DNA. She moved heaven and earth to make the courts exhume Sarita's body, which was buried in the cemetery next to her brother and baby niece, and they tested it. They took some of Sara's blood. The result was negative. They repeated the test, and again the result was negative.

Soon after that, her brother-in-law received a mysterious phone call claiming Sarita was in a brothel in Valladolid, Spain.

I think Olivero sold her to a trafficking ring, to get rid of her, Sara says.

But Mirta shakes her head.

If my sister were alive, she'd have come back. I don't know how, but even if she'd been kidnapped, she would have found a way to escape and come back. She wouldn't have abandoned us. She wouldn't have left her son. Those bones aren't hers, but my sister is dead as well.

Mirta says *as well* and then it hits me that there's another dead woman who no one's making a fuss about, or whose family are still searching for her: that bundle of bones buried in Sarita's name.

Germán, the son of Sarita Mundín, is now a grown man and has children of his own. His grandmother and aunt are proud of him, of having made sure he studied and finished secondary school. Although he was unlucky and married a wastrel, says Sara, a girl who left him for another man. He never asks about his mother, or even mentions her.

He takes after me there, says Mirta. We're private people. No one at work knows she's my sister. Every now and then something comes out, something in the paper that reminds people. Everyone knows about her case, it's been talked about so much. If anyone asks if we're related, I say no. I don't want people knowing she's my sister, I don't want any more questions. My pain is mine and I don't want to share it. It's only her, my mum, who keeps going with it all.

Two years after this conversation, I found out that Germán was in prison, in Detention Facility 5 in Villa María, for possession of drugs.

There's never any sign of Sarita in the tarot, either alive or dead. She's the only one of the three who never speaks. The Señora says she feels that Sarita is alive, or at least that she was until recently.

As well as the negative DNA test, her mother has an almost occult reason for believing Sarita is alive: I've never been able to dream about her, she says. I would have liked to touch her again, to hear that voice I can no longer remember, even if it were only a dream. But then, I think if I've never dreamed about her it must be because she's still alive. If she were dead, she'd have come back in a dream to say goodbye.

When I leave Sara's, the afternoon is still cold, gloomy and deserted. The taxi driver is waiting for me, parked opposite the house. He's listening to a football match. The broadcast is interrupted now and then by the crackling of the taxi radio, the voice of a young woman who, from the little central office, reels off customers' names and addresses.

Since 1977 in Villa María, some twenty unpunished murders have been recorded. In 2002, the femicide of Mariela La Condorito López led to the formation of the Truth and Justice Organisation, which later became Real Truth, Justice for All.

La Condorito, a mentally disabled prostitute, was found with her throat cut, wrapped in a blanket, on a piece of wasteland in the city. She had links to the Sister Adorers congregation, which ran a scheme for getting girls off the streets and teaching them a trade. The nuns protected them, and La Condorito was an old friend of the convent. When she was murdered, the sisters Beatriz and Albeana decided they had to do something, that their congregation and the whole Villa María community had to take a stand. They founded the organisation to raise awareness and support the victims' families.

Before La Condorito, the taxi driver Mónica Leocato was found raped and strangled in her car, on a country road, seemingly by a customer. A brutal crime that remains unpunished. And a few years later, in 2005, Mariela Bessonart disappeared. The last person who saw her, and the only suspect in her disappearance, is her ex-husband and the father of her children.

Raúl Favre was the Danne family doctor. He wasn't particularly surprised when he heard knocking at his door just after one that morning. Small-town doctors are used to their patients showing up at their homes at all hours of the day or night. When he opened the door he found Eymar Danne and another man, who was introduced as a neighbour. Danne told him something was wrong with his daughter Andrea, and he had to come and see her right away. Since it was still raining, Favre decided to take the car in case he had to drive the girl to hospital or sort out anything else.

When he went into the bedroom, he saw the girl lying in bed, with a large pool of dried blood on her chest and blood on the floor by the side of the bed. Her mother was sitting on the bed next to hers, as if frozen, and barely seemed to register his arrival. Danne, meanwhile, was very agitated and asked him several times if his daughter was dead.

Is she dead? Is she dead? Is she dead?

Yes, she's dead.

Well then, that's fine, she's dead now, there's nothing more we can do, the doctor said he heard her father say.

Realising he couldn't do anything for the girl either, the doctor offered to go and get the police. They didn't have a phone in the house.

It was a long rest of the night in which relatives, friends and curious bystanders gathered in Andrea's room, looking at her laid out in bed and covered in blood.

The dance at the Santa Rosa club was the point the news spread from. Fabiana Danne was there with some friends. Her brother went to find her and tell her to come home because Andrea had had an accident. Some friends went back with her, and other people she knew followed behind. Then came relatives who lived on the same block, like the grandmother, an aunt, some cousins. And soon after that, the boyfriend and the boyfriend's parents.

All traipsing in and out of that bedroom. The more squeamish peering from the doorway.

A murder in the privacy of a family home, which had the same exposure as a death by the roadside.

At some point the house became so crowded that the police decided to remove the body. They took it to the morgue without waiting for the Grey Lion, the only photographer in town, who, as well as social occasions, stepped in to document accidents and, from time to time, corpses. There are no photos of Andrea Danne in the case file. Only pictures of the empty scene, with her body gone, and bloodstains on the floor and the mattress.

The autopsy report says:

Death occurred at approximately 1 a.m. on November 16th, 1986.

Death was caused by acute anaemia caused by a massive haemorrhage caused by a wound in the right atrium.

The wound was effected by a knife or similar object, slim, with a blade around 3 cm wide and at least 8 cm to 10 cm long, which was inserted with the blade pointing towards the distal part of the body.

When the act occurred, Miss Danne would have been asleep, in a supine position and with the attacker most likely to her right, and the weapon in the attacker's right hand.

No further injuries or signs of external violence are recorded. No evidence was found on her hands to suggest a struggle or an attempt to defend herself upon being attacked.

It is likely that the assailant was an adult, who operated the weapon with some force and speed.

Doctor Favre was one of the first people to see Andrea's body lying face-up, her hands by her sides, perfectly clean, her arms extended and resting on the bedspread, which covered her up to the waist. There was a lot of dried blood on her chest, dried blood in the gap between her arm and her body, and blood on the floor. Her death had been almost instantaneous, presumably occurring in the time the haemorrhage lasted, a couple of minutes or so.

When he was called to testify, they read him the autopsy report and asked if the position the girl's body was found in was consistent with the way she was murdered. The doctor said no.

The mortal wound, as it's described in the coroner's report, injured the large blood vessels and the right atrium of the heart, but it's a shallow lesion, in an area of low blood pressure, which means the haemorrhage resulting from the wound isn't massive. The victim takes around two minutes to die. Enough time to make movements, because the blood goes on reaching the brain through the blood vessels that aren't injured. Voluntary movements at first and then involuntary ones, when the blood pressure drops due to the haemorrhage. The body would have been partly curled up and the bed would have been in disarray. I think someone arranged the body before I got there, he said.

In the eighties, my mum worked as a nurse at a clinic in my town. Doctor Favre was on the medical team. In the downtime on their shifts, they'd often discuss Andrea's murder. For the doctor there was one unanswered question, which he went over endlessly in his mind: how could the murderer have got into the house, killed the girl, taken the time to arrange her body so it looked like she was asleep, and then left again, without the mother or father or little brother, who slept in the next room, on the other side of the wall, with a door connecting the two rooms, hearing anything at all?

Favre died some years ago. His eternal question, unanswered.

The friends, relatives and curious bystanders in Andrea's bedroom didn't include sixteen-year-old Aldo Cettour, a neighbour and distant cousin of the victim, who would later become another suspect.

Aldo was late to everything that night: late to the dance at the Santa Rosa club, arriving just as Fabiana and the others were hurrying out following the news of Andrea's accident, and too late to see his neighbour's corpse.

When he came back from the dance in the early hours, his parents and sister were still up. The three of them had been at the Dannes' house and they told him what they saw there. Aldo made for the front door, intending to go round too, not wanting to miss the scene people would be talking about for years to come. But his mother stopped him. She said they'd already taken the girl away and there was no reason to go, there was nothing left to see. Not even blood, because after the people from the morgue removed the body, Fabiana had started cleaning. She collected bucket after bucket of water and blood and tipped them into the yard.

A few months earlier, Aldo and some friends had

snuck onto the Dannes' patio down a little path that linked his backyard to theirs, and spied on Andrea and Fabiana through their bedroom window as they were getting ready for bed. The girls caught them and there was a bit of a row. Some of their underwear had also gone missing from the clothes line.

In my town there was an incurable peeping tom, Bochita Aguilera, a dumpy, moustached man in his fifties who lived alone with his mother. He was a master baker and in the evenings, on the way home from work, he slipped into the open yards of the houses to spy on the girls through the thin gauzy curtains people used to have. He was harmless. He just liked feasting his eyes on those beautiful young bodies moving around in the bedrooms, getting ready for bed. Every now and then, a house dog or one of the girls would spot him *in flagrante* and Bochita would make a run for it, before the father of the outraged girl could catch him.

On the night of the crime, Aldo was playing pool with a friend in the nearby town of Colón. It was past midnight and he could see there was a storm on the way, so he decided to hitchhike back to San José. The wind and rain caught him as he waited by the roadside, out in the open. By the time a car stopped, he was soaked through. He got home and changed his clothes. It was still early for bed, so he went out again, to the dance at the club, a few blocks away. On his way in, he passed Fabiana and some of her friends, who were rushing out looking shell-shocked. I can't believe it, I can't believe it, he heard one of them say.

Not until he stepped into the hall, where the dance was still going on as the whispers of Andrea's death began to spread, through the music, the cigarette smoke, the glasses of beer, not until that moment, did someone tell him his neighbour had been stabbed.

As well as spying on the girls, Aldo had seen a psychologist for a few months. Three decades ago, in a town like San José, seeing a therapist was practically the same as being crazy. He'd been treated because, according to the case file, he'd been feeling weird and shutting himself away. He never felt like that again afterwards.

Aldo and his mates' teenage prank doesn't seem like solid grounds for suspecting him of murder. But with the investigation going round in circles, and no proof to speak of, everyone, in a way, was a suspect.

Remember the kid who stole their knickers? Paula says, and bursts out laughing. Eduardo just smiles. Maybe he doesn't think it's funny, or maybe he doesn't remember.

We're sitting in a conservatory full of plants, overlooking a garden with soft green grass, even though it's only August. It's a sunny afternoon.

Paula is the mother of Eduardo Germanier, the boyfriend Andrea had when she was killed. She's a talkative woman, energetic and quick to laughter. Every time she laughs her cheeks lift and her sky-blue eyes vanish behind her glasses. She's going to leave us alone for the time it takes to get the *mate* from the house next door, where she lives with her husband. The house with the conservatory where we're sitting, and the other houses built on the same land, are rented to the tourists who choose Colón as a holiday or long-weekend destination, for its river and thermal baths. As a mother of only boys, Paula is something of a mother hen and sometimes jumps in before Eduardo can open his mouth, or murmurs things to me under her breath. She's probably overprotective of all her children, but especially this one, who ten years ago was struggling to recover from a stroke that almost killed him. The stroke took away some parts of his memory. Although Paula repeatedly tells me how well he remembers what happened with Andrea, there are obviously some stories they've rehearsed together before I arrived. She hovers close by, ready to prompt him when his memory fails, when he falls silent and stares out at the garden, trying to piece the memories together or searching for the right words, because the stroke also left him with a slight speech impediment. Now and then he gets flustered by his overeager mother and tells her to be patient, to let him work out what he wants to say, that we'll come to that bit later.

The Germanier family lived for a few years in the suburbs of Buenos Aires. Not long after they returned to Colón, where they're originally from, Eduardo met Andrea at the house of some mutual friends. He had long hair and rode a motorbike. He's always been into bikes, though he's had several serious accidents. After the stroke he had to give them up, but he still misses them. He says now he just looks at them online.

You see me like this now, but you have no idea what I used to be like.

I don't confess this yet, but I remember him being very handsome as a young man. He still is. I have a vague recollection of seeing his photo in the paper, on one of those marches organised at the time to demand justice for Andrea. I remember the long curly hair, and people saying he'd sworn not to cut it until his girlfriend's murder was solved.

He liked her the moment he saw her. She was gorgeous. And two or three weeks after they met, he asked her to be his girl, as people said then. They were boyfriend and girlfriend. He tells me they had a wonderful relationship, that they got on well together, that he really loved her.

The night of the murder, they went for a ride on the motorbike and when they got back they started kissing and cuddling in the kitchen. Everyone else was in bed. At one point they heard some noises outside and he went to see what was going on. He looked out onto the patio and over at the garage where Andrea's father kept his car, but he saw nothing. He was a bit scared. In time, he came to think those noises he heard were Andrea's mother, spying on her daughter. It had happened once before: they'd caught her watching them through the kitchen window. Her parents' bedroom had two doors, one leading to the girls' bedroom and the other out to the front of the house. So she could go through that door and get into the backyard, round the side way.

He's told me that various times, Paula backs him up.

They were silent for a while, listening hard, and when they didn't hear anything else they kissed some more, stringing out their farewell, which would come sooner than usual that evening because Andrea had to study.

Eduardo rode home with the storm at his heels. For the last few miles, the wind was up and seemed almost about to lift him off his bike. He arrived as the first drops were falling and went straight to bed.

It was ten to midnight, I remember it well because I heard the door and looked at the time, Paula says. I was awake. I'd been in bed all day, with women's troubles, you know, and I couldn't sleep. I heard him come in and go to his room. A few hours later I heard knocking. The storm had subsided, but it was still raining. A knocking at the door and a woman's voice calling: Eduardo, Eduardo, let me in, please. I thought it was Andrea, that she'd had a fight with my son and he'd left her out there. I don't know, I didn't understand. From my bed I shouted: Coming, Andrea, I'm coming. But what happened, my God, did Eduardo leave you outside...? When I opened the door, it wasn't her. I saw a girl standing there who I'd never seen before. I'm Andrea's sister, she said, Andrea's had an accident, Eduardo has to come to my house. By then, my husband was at the door as well, all the commotion had woken him up. I went in to wake Eduardo, to tell him to get dressed because we had to go to San José. My husband carried on talking to Fabiana, and she told him Andrea had been killed. But we, Eduardo and I, had no idea. When we got there, Andrea's father was waiting for us outside. That was the first time we'd met him, my husband and I didn't know her parents. He introduced himself and lit the way to the house with a torch because there was water and mud everywhere. It was only once we were in the room that the penny dropped and we realised she was dead.

Eduardo's distress when he saw his girlfriend's lifeless body, and the room covered in blood, was terrible to see. He started yelling, punching the walls. A few people managed to restrain him and drag him into the kitchen to calm him down.

I freaked out, he says, staring into the distance. He has his mother's sky-blue eyes.

But in the kitchen he went on sobbing and screaming.

There were several women in there, Paula remembers. I was trying to comfort him, but I was also thinking of Andrea and her mother. I was thinking of that poor woman, what she must be going through. We'd never met, remember. I assumed they'd taken her to a neighbour or something. The women there were all so calm. And then one of them comes over to Eduardo and tells him to please be quiet, to stop shouting, because he's upsetting

Andrea's grandmother, who was an old lady. That's when I saw red. Who did she think she was, talking to my son like that when he was going through hell. And who might this be? I asked out loud. And another of the women said: It's Gloria, it's Andrea's mum. I couldn't believe it: her daughter was dead and she was worrying about the grandmother... Honest to God!

That's Paula's first memory of Andrea's mother and from that point on she couldn't stand her. It wasn't, she thought, how a woman should act when her daughter has just been killed. So calm. For that, Paula has never forgiven her.

Eduardo's relationship with his girlfriend's parents was fairly distant. Gloria had rarely broken her silence: that night, when she asked him to be quiet, and the odd time in the past when she asked him about his work, if he was a salaried employee, if they covered his social insurance contributions. Eduardo never understood where these questions were leading, and nor did he give it much thought. He spoke to Andrea's father a little more, but only what was right and necessary.

Those were different times. It wasn't the same friendly relationship kids have with adults nowadays, he says.

Meanwhile, Andrea got on very well with Eduardo's family. Paula was extremely fond of her and approved of the relationship. Whenever Andrea came to visit, she lent a hand in the little shop they had; if there were lots of customers, she'd start serving them without having to be asked. They helped her pay for her studies. And they also helped with the funeral costs.

Paula and Eduardo's memory of that night and the crime scene doesn't match the recollections of the expert witnesses recorded in the case file, or of the other witnesses.

They describe the kitchen as carnage: bloodstains on the walls, the table askew, one drawer hanging open, kitchen knives all over the place. And then more blood on the bedroom walls and doors. As if there'd been a ferocious struggle across the two rooms. They think it was a fight between mother and daughter, and that, in a fit of madness, Gloria stabbed Andrea.

When I tell them that according to the autopsy report, Andrea was stabbed in her bed as she slept, and that her body showed no other signs of violence or of her having defended herself from her attacker, Paula shakes her head, indignant.

No, that's impossible. Impossible. Andrea was killed by her mother. So what you're saying can't be right.

Why not?

Because, my dear, a mother couldn't kill her daughter like that.

Eduardo was also a suspect in his girlfriend's murder. The first suspect.

Andrea's sister admits, in her court testimony, that when she heard her sister had been killed, she thought right away that it must have been Eduardo, because he was jealous and possessive. That's why she went to his house herself to get him. But when she saw his reaction to her sister's corpse, she realised she was wrong.

Paula also realised, that same night, that they'd try to blame her son. To this day, she insists that everything was set up to point the finger at Eduardo. That's why the family got in touch with their lawyer as soon as possible. She never doubted his innocence, of course. But Eduardo's father did. There was a hesitation, a moment of uncertainty Eduardo noticed when his dad went out to check his motorbike, looking for traces of who knows what. But he doubted him, and although it was more than twenty years ago, and although there are some things Eduardo can't remember after his stroke, he's never forgotten that. And it still hurts.

He's always carried that with him, Paula tells me, unnecessarily.

As well as having the best lawyer in the city, Eduardo's family hired a private detective. They were sure the police would want to lock the boy up as soon as possible and wash their hands of the case. But the detective failed to provide any new information or firm leads. The police and the judge hounded Eduardo for months, before eventually leaving him in peace. The investigation was dissolving, in spite of the silent marches he organised with Andrea's friends, and which the dead girl's family never attended.

I tell him I vaguely remember seeing a photo of him on one of those marches, and people saying he wasn't going to cut his hair until his girlfriend's murderer was found. I tell him I was a teenager at the time and fell in love with that declaration – and with him, of course.

He laughs. He says he doesn't remember, but it's possible, he might have promised that. But now I can see he didn't keep his word, he adds.

About six years later he met the woman who's now his wife and the mother of his children. One way or another, he understood that life went on.

When I tell him I went to Andrea's tomb, he asks me if his plaque is still there. Yes, it's there. It's a simple plaque and it says:

> My love for you is eternal.
> Your boyfriend, Eduardo.

The violent death of a young person, in a small community, is always a shock. The news of María Luisa Quevedo's murder was covered, almost from the outset, with fantastical flourishes by the local press. It took a couple of days to appear, as a tiny piece in *Norte*, the biggest newspaper in Chaco province. Headlined Mysterious Death of Underage Girl, it sat alongside another: Underage Boy Missing.

At first, the so-called Quevedo Case had to compete with matters taking up the agenda of the new democratic government and its citizens' attention: the theft of babies and children during the dictatorship, the discovery of unidentified bodies in the Sáenz Peña cemetery, the first summons of military leaders to give evidence in court over kidnappings and disappearances in the period 1976-1982.

But it soon gained space and prominence, becoming the number one mystery and horror series of that 1984 Chaco summer. A tale of intrigue, suspicion, red herrings and false testimony, which people followed in the papers and on the radio as if it were a soap opera or a serialised novel.

There were no immediate results, the court recess was coming up, the investigating judge in charge, Dr Díaz Colodrero, was a commercial judge with no criminal experience, one of the policemen involved was tainted by the vices of the dictatorship – all this meant the case got bogged down over the summer and became fuel for the press, which, in the absence of fresh developments, covered rumours, gossip and neighbours' suppositions.

María Luisa's death turned into a witch hunt and people were going in and out of the court, showing up to testify of their own accord and naming guilty parties left, right and centre. Every day these accusations were amplified by the press and taken as firm leads which, by the next day, had crumbled due to lack of concrete proof.

Two employees of Don Gómez, the septuagenarian bus magnate who the family still identify as the sole culprit. Gómez himself. María Luisa's two new friends, one of whom was even nicknamed Foxy. Two boys from respected families in the city. A young woman who lived in the same neighbourhood as the victim. An indigenous man with the surname Vega who, according to the newspaper, was found in a terrible state, wandering through the same waste ground where the girl's body had been left, and who died in hospital a few days later. They all had their share of newsprint as the coverage rolled on.

There were days when the María Luisa murder case appeared as a short article in between other, more important stories, days when it filled a quarter of a page, and others when it had a full page, complete with a photo. Or if not a photo, a pencil sketch of the suspect, or even of María Luisa herself. This gallery of presumed murderers and accomplices went on to include the police officers accused of beating witnesses to obtain false testimony, who were swiftly sent away on leave until it all blew over.

María Luisa's relatives have a constant, central role. The absent father, an ex-boxer, demanding the mystery of his daughter's death be resolved immediately. An extremely young Yogui Quevedo, leaning against a shelf of televisions and looking straight at the camera; the photo was probably taken in the appliance repair shop where he worked at the time.

Some articles claimed the murder happened on the

same patch of wasteland where the girl's body was found. Others, that her body was dragged there and marks were visible on the ground. Another, that she was killed in the shack where Vega the indigenous man lived: in this scenario, his death soon after the crime, from Chagas disease, would be a kind of divine punishment. Another, that she was strangled but not raped. Another, that she was thrown into the reservoir when she was still alive and then drowned. Another, that she wasn't raped, but already had an active sex life. And, of course, the romantic version, which claimed that María Luisa had been seeing a married man, who'd ended things that very day, leaving the girl, devastated by the break-up, wandering the streets in the centre of Sáenz Peña at the mercy of her captors.

The media frenzy around the case infected the parents of teenage girls with paranoia. In a piece published almost a month after the crime, the newspaper *Norte* wonders: Do parents have no awareness in a community like this one, which claims to be organised? We know we can't expect anything from the murderer or murderers, after what they did. But are the different sectors of the population not capable of raising their voice in protest and finding a more effective way to respond? Will our children no longer be able to walk the city's streets with an easy mind?

The story of Yogui Quevedo, María Luisa's brother and spokesperson, also strays, at points, into telenovela terrain. The perfect murderer will always be Jesús Gómez, the rich, powerful man who held parties to lure in young girls and seduced them with his wealth. Yogui's sister, the honest, hard-working girl, the maid from Monseñor de Carlo, a poor neighbourhood in Sáenz Peña, who spurned Gómez' romantic advances and ended up dead, sullied by the lecherous tycoon. And Yogui the avenger, the incorruptible man who refused the briefcases of cash he was sent by Gómez' messengers. For a while after my sister died I went around like a madman, a gun in my belt the whole time. I'd sworn to my baby sister, to my baby sister's memory, that I was going to shoot Don Gómez. A woman I was with back then came up with a plan. She was stunning, and since she knew the old man liked girls, she was going to pick the old codger up, take him to a motel, and then, when they were both in bed, I could burst in and blow his brains out, simple as. But it never happened. I was totally up for it. It seemed so simple. And it was the only way of justice being done, because meanwhile Don Gómez was going around using money to cover everything up, buying witnesses, lawyers… What stopped me was La Doña, the Paraguayan psychic we went to see when my sister disappeared. I carried on seeing her after that, consulting her about everything to do with my baby sister's death, and I really started to believe her because I had to hold onto something. And she convinced me to let go of the idea of killing someone. She convinced me that I was the only one who'd suffer, because I'd end up rotting in jail. That it wasn't worth getting my hands dirty, that the guilty people were going to pay. And pay they did. Two of them, in the end. Don Gómez died poor and alone, his family all disowned him after what happened and he lost his entire fortune, the lawyers walked away with everything. And the other guy I think was behind it, the one who chatted up my baby sister, Francisco Suárez, the guy she was talking to on the pavement the last time I saw her alive, he died too. In an accident. Some people were travelling in a truck that overturned and he was the only one who died. So at least divine justice did me right.

Although he put down his gun, swayed by the Paraguayan, he still ended up with a bullet in his leg. He says he was going home one morning in the early hours and a stripped-down car, all chassis, drove past him on a corner and the people in it fired some shots at him. One bullet wounded him in the leg. Years later, working as a refuse collector, he saw the same car abandoned in a garage. He's sure it was the same one, but he has no proof, and even though he reported it to the police, nothing ever came of it.

But the fantastical events in Yogui Quevedo's tale don't end there. After the attack, the threats, the extortion and his plans to liquidate Gómez, there was something else. The story he tells me could be a scene from a Raymond Chandler novel.

One day, a beautiful woman turns up at the house where he still lives with his mother and younger sister, asking for him. He comes to the door and the woman says she's an undercover agent from the police force in Resistencia. She introduces herself as Leo. She says she has a taxi waiting, and there is indeed a taxi in the street outside. She says she wants to talk to him, that she has information for him about his sister's murder, but that right now she's due back in Resistencia and can she come the next day. They arrange to meet in the late afternoon. She'll come and pick him up.

The next day, Leo shows up just as they'd agreed. She asks if they can go to his room, where they'll be more comfortable. They close the door behind them. It's a scorching day, and the woman says she's very sweaty and would he mind if she gets changed. She has a fresh outfit in her bag. He says of course, that's fine, he can show her to the bathroom if she likes. She says there's no need, she can change right there while they talk. Soon she's standing naked in front of him. He says she had a beautiful body. All of her was beautiful. And he lets her do it. Take all her clothes off, end up naked, completely naked, he clarifies, then get dressed again. After that, he suggests they go to the cinema.

Going to the cinema is part of another plan. A plan Yogui has to foil the woman's plan.

After Leo's first visit, Yogui can't relax, so he goes to the local police station and tells the officers working on his sister's case that this woman came to see him, claiming to be an undercover agent. They check with the police in Resistencia, but there's no officer with that name. Leo is an impostor. He tells them they'd arranged to meet the next day. So they plot her capture. Yogui will take her to the cinema and the police will ambush them, then drive them both off in separate police cars on the pretext of checking their records. He'll be let go, and she'll be taken to the police station for questioning.

And that's what happens. After having her naked in his room, Yogui takes her to the cinema and the police spring into action.

Eventually he learnt she was the secretary at a major law firm in Resistencia. They sent her to find out how much I knew, because they were Don Gómez' lawyers. One time, back then, I called the firm and asked for her. I said I was her cousin. But they told me she didn't work there any more, he says.

The murder of Andrea Danne, too, has a second chapter that's clearly straight from fiction. An event that leads, ten years after her murder, to the case being reopened.

In August 1995 in Concepción del Uruguay, the nearest city to Andrea's town, a girl of eighteen, María Laura Voeffray, is detained on drug charges. When this happens, the girl announces that she knows who killed Andrea Danne.

And she tells this story.

At the time of the murder, she was ten years old. She lived in a little house in El Brillante, a small town just outside San José, almost a suburb of the city. That night, when her parents are asleep, María Laura sneaks out through a window, grabs her bicycle and goes off with three other girls her age to ride around the centre of San José. At some point her bike gets a puncture, so she decides to leave it at a petrol station, in the area for pumping up tyres. She leaves it propped against a wall and splits off from the group, ending up alone. She carries on walking around and her aimless wandering takes her to where Andrea lives, just as the storm is breaking. When she passes the Dannes' house, she sees a big maroon car parked outside. There's a man in the driver's seat but the car isn't moving, and the lights and engine are turned off. For some reason, she has a bad feeling about this car and hides in some bushes at the front of the house. From her hiding place, and in spite of the rain and wind, she hears the sound of something like cardboard being slashed with a knife, and a muffled scream, a moan. Then she sees two men emerge from the back of the house, down a passage between it and the house next door. One is wearing a dark suit. It's a clear night, she says, in spite of the storm. She recognises the man in the suit, it's Jim Shaw, a shopkeeper of Chinese descent, very well-known in the city. Behind him is a blonde guy of around twenty, who she doesn't recognise. Jim Shaw and the blonde guy pause a moment some five yards from her hiding place. Then she clearly sees the Chinese man hand the blonde guy a knife covered in blood. She remembers it was very thin and long, like a dagger. The blonde guy wraps the weapon in a handkerchief. Come on, come on, says Jim Shaw, getting into the car next to his companion. The blonde guy looks for a branch then retraces his steps, using the branch to sweep the ground and hide his tracks. He opens the back door of the car and gets in, rubbing away the tracks he's just left. The car starts and they disappear.

María Laura climbs out of the bushes, feeling curious and perhaps slightly uneasy about the whole situation. She walks round the house and goes in the back way. The window to the yard has its shutters half-open, so she peers through and sees Andrea Danne lying in bed, her hands on her chest, covered in blood and with blood on the sheets and the floor. There are no lights on in the house, but she can still make out the scene in detail because, she repeats, it's a clear night in spite of the storm. Eventually, she sees a light go on in another room and runs away, afraid, and doesn't stop running until she gets home and climbs in through the window she slipped out of several hours before.

She never told anyone because she was terrified. Or rather, she told a few police officer friends recently and they said she should present herself and testify, but she never wanted to. She admits to being romantically involved with Jim Shaw a couple of years ago. Faced with the judge's incredulity – how could she have had a relationship with someone she suspected was a murderer? – María Laura explains that she's a single mother and Jim gave her money, and that it's not the only time she's gone out with a man for cash. That she has no choice. At one point in that relationship, which didn't last long, she told Jim people were saying he'd killed the Danne girl. She said it to test him, to see how he'd react. According to her, the Chinese man was taken aback and said that's what folks get for talking too much. María Laura, unperturbed, answered that you hear all kinds of things about the place. And Jim Shaw ended the conversation by saying we're slaves to the words we speak and masters of those we don't, and that what would she know about who killed the Danne girl.

The case was reopened after the girl's statement. Jim Shaw was summoned, questioned, investigated and then let go.

The crime that, in 1986, hadn't spread beyond the local press, caught the attention of national papers like *Crónica* and *Clarín*.

In characteristic style, *Crónica* used the headline: Chinaman Goes Down Nine Years After Murder. And when Shaw went free: Chinaman Victim of Scorned Young Lover.

Enrique Sdrech, the famous crime reporter, travelled to Entre Ríos and wrote a full-page piece for the Sunday edition of *Clarín*. He slipped in a possible motive: that Jim Shaw dealt drugs in the area and Andrea, aware what was going on, had threatened to report him. He also says the Chinese shopkeeper had a violent reputation, and that the neighbours recalled how once, annoyed with his fourteen-year-old daughter, he threw her out of her bedroom window, which was on the first floor.

The memory came back to life.

However, María Laura Voeffray's story was no more than that: a story made up by a lying girl with an overactive imagination who just wanted to save her own skin.

María Luisa loved this brother very much, the Señora tells me. She's happy to have him as her spokesman. She's happy he found this role for himself after her murder. And I'll tell you something else: she doesn't want it to be resolved. The day it's resolved is the day he's left with nothing more to say.

The siblings, in these three cases, play a fundamental role. Yogui Quevedo is the spokesman for his murdered little sister, he's become a public figure after María Luisa's death and is consulted every time there's a similar case in Chaco province. Mirta Mundín was Sarita's confidante, her protégée, and the one who raised her disappeared sister's son. She prefers not to speak in public, not to reveal her pain, which is hers alone, something intimate that she defends tooth and nail. And Fabiana, Andrea Danne's sister, now prefers to remain silent.

In the article Enrique Sdrech writes for *Clarín*, on September 10th 1995, there's a special inset box about Fabiana. It's headed The Sister's Promise. And it says:

When María Andrea Danne was killed nine years ago, the most outlandish theories did the rounds in San José. Many people saw the shadowy hand of a cult behind the murder, or of drugs, or prostitution, and suspicion even fell on the victim's own father, Eymar Pablo Danne.

For a long time afterwards, María Fabiana, María Andrea's sister, was said to have behaved 'strangely' in mopping the floor and washing the bloodstained clothes. 'What people don't realise is that I had permission to do it from the police officer on duty at my house. I always dreamed of studying law, qualifying as a lawyer and going back through the file on my sister's murder. Now I've qualified and I know the file off by heart and I won't rest until the case is resolved,' Mariana Fabiana, who has just turned twenty-six, told *Clarín*.

Fabiana never agreed to an interview with me, only to answer a short email questionnaire around three years ago, when I was just beginning my fieldwork. After that, all my emails and calls to her law firm went unanswered. This is what she said to me then:

Andrea and I got on really well, we confided in each other, though after she got a boyfriend we didn't always go around together or share all the same friends. I don't remember much of what happened on the day she died. For years I remembered it intensely, minute by minute, but nothing ever stood out as unusual. But then, I was organising the school prom and would have been busy all that day, so maybe I wouldn't have noticed even if there had been anything strange. Still, I can't imagine her having a problem and not telling me. She definitely wouldn't have told our parents, because they were strict and uptight. They never hit us, but a look or a simple no were enough. They didn't want us having boyfriends. It didn't stop Andrea, but I never dared bring anyone home. I found out what happened because my twelve-year-old brother came with a neighbour to get me, at the dance I was at, a couple of blocks from home. Andrea's had an accident, they said. It was raining and the three of us ran back to the house. The whole time I was thinking she and her boyfriend had had a motorbike accident. I was really scared. I sensed it was serious, but I never imagined what was coming. When I got there, my mum took me by the shoulders and told me Andrea was dead. I don't remember her exact words, but I remember her anguished expression. I can't keep remembering because what happened that night destroys me, even after so long. At first I thought her boyfriend might have killed her, because he was extremely jealous, that's why I wanted to be the one to go and get him, and I even said I blamed him. But when I saw his reaction to the body, I didn't think it could have been him. We had no more contact with him or his family after that. A few years ago we ran into each other and said hello, but we didn't mention what happened.

My life was never the same after my sister's death. My parents went to pieces, with my mum depressed and my dad very withdrawn. And my brother, who was twelve,

As a girl I loved going to the cemetery. On sunny afternoons, on winter Sundays, with bags of chrysanthemums
or dahlias, flowers my gran grew in her garden with the
sole purpose of adorning the graves of our dead. Summer
Sundays, too, but in the early morning, before the sun
came beating down on our heads, when the cypresses
lining the main avenue still gave off a fresh cool scent and
the burial niches and tombs cast their shadows on the
graves below. I took other seasonal flowers in the bags,
and always carnations and pinks, which last longer, which
don't give in so easily, so meekly to the heat. And sprigs
of sword fern, which also endure.

Two tombs in particular fascinated and scared me, in
a dark, romantic way that for a girl of seven or eight was
impossible to explain. They were two tombs in opposite
niches, facing one another. In the first, a young woman
who died of an illness. In the second, a youth barely older
than her, who died in an accident. Her picture was a
studio portrait, the kind women in the 1940s or 1950s sat
for once in their lives, before their wedding photo. His
was a photo from an ID card, showing him serious and
with very short hair, probably because he was an army
conscript at the time.

I don't know if I was told this or if I made it up, but
I remember I liked to look at them because they'd been
courting before they died. Death took her first. And it
came for him soon after. That's what the dates on the
bronze plaques said. I think I must have got the part
about the illness and the accident from the epitaphs, too.
I never left the cemetery without paying them a visit. I'd

stand in between them, but a few steps away, so it seemed like the two photos were looking at each other. And I felt there was no greater love than that of this pair, who for a long time now had been no more than love-struck dust.

I think my relationship with death was far more natural in my childhood. Perhaps because we'd been told that the father of my cousin, who was like a twin brother to me, had died in an accident before either of us were born. Or because many of our dogs and cats died prematurely, crossing the road, hit by trucks. Or because a neighbour's little boy had died that way, too; and a girl at my school; and another neighbour, a boy, Buey Martín, who came off his motorbike after a dance. Back then, death wasn't only for the old and sick. I'd hear people saying that so-and-so had died in the flower of youth and I thought it was a beautiful image.

Then my views changed. I don't know exactly when or why, but I began to be afraid. I stopped going to the cemetery because at night I dreamt the dead were coming after me.

Somehow, my meetings with the Señora changed those feelings. The afternoons we spent together were like those afternoon trips to the cemetery. A kind of reconciliation.

A taxi driver agrees, begrudgingly, to take me to the outskirts of Sáenz Peña. It's midday and the sun is splitting above us like a ripe cheese. The guy would rather be at home by now than crossing the city, dodging the packs of scooters that buzz along, clogging the full width of the roads. On the way I try to convince him to wait for me, just for a bit, fifteen minutes at most, but he says no. No, lady, I'm already off duty, but I'll send a car later if you like. I say yes, though I doubt he'll send anyone, or that anyone will want to come at this hour, when everyone's going to sleep, when the city is dying until five o'clock.

Where shall I drop you? he asks when we're arriving.

Here's fine.

He brakes near the intersection of Calle 51 and Calle 28. While I'm paying, I try again.

Sure you can't wait just a little?

Madam, I've already told you, I'm off duty. I shouldn't even have brought you this far, honestly.

I haven't finished closing the door and already he's making a U-turn and disappearing at full speed in a cloud of dust.

To one side of me there's a social housing development. Identical little houses, all painted white, blinding where they reflect the sun. All with identical water tanks on the roof.

On the other side, a rubbish tip. A shimmering swamp, blue and green from the flies. A dog, every now and then, nosing around in the piles of trash. It smells foul.

The other two corners of the intersection are empty lots, covered in weeds.

María Luisa Quevedo's body was thrown into one of these four bits of land, but which?

I look around, a bit disoriented. There's no one here. In some places, noon feels more frightening than the dead of night. For something to do, I take a few photos with a little camera I have in my rucksack. I don't know why, the landscape's grim and desolate. I tell myself it's so I can remember it later, but I know I'll never download the photos, that most likely I'll delete them or lose them.

As I'm doing that, I hear a voice behind me.

Go on, take more, take more, let the governor see the squalor he's got us living in.

A woman is on her way home, her house is right on

the corner, and she's wheeling her bike. She seems to think I'm a journalist.

I walk over and say hello. She's a young woman, slim and energetic.

Are you taking pictures for the paper?

No. But maybe you can help me. I'm looking for where a girl's body was left, some years ago. I don't know if you remember. Was it here, in the rubbish tip?

Maira Tévez? Yeah, right there, they threw her on that tip there.

The murder of Maira Tévez is more recent, though the papers were also quick to link it to María Luisa Quevedo. Maira was twenty-one, and training to be an English teacher. In 2010, her boyfriend, Héctor Ponce, shot her in the head and then cut her body into pieces and deposited them in different places: the arms and legs went in the septic tank of the apartment block where the girl lived; the head was most likely thrown into some wasteland and then dragged by dogs into the yard of a neighbour, who reported it; the torso was found on this rubbish tip.

No, I'm asking about another girl: María Luisa Quevedo. Was her body left there too?

Oh, no. They put the Quevedo girl over there.

She points to one of the patches of scrubland.

My husband found her...

Your husband found the body?

Yeah, my mother-in-law's always talking about that story.

He's not in, by any chance? I'd like to speak to him.

Yeah, he's here. Actually, hang on a second, I'll ask him. Is it for the paper?

No, I'm writing a book...

The woman nods and goes through a door to what looks like a concrete patio. She soon reappears and invites me in.

The house is in semi-darkness, with all the shutters closed and a floor fan that barely shifts the air.

With the flies and everything we have to keep it all closed, she tells me.

When my eyes adjust, I make out a man sitting at the table with a baby girl in his lap, who he's feeding.

We say hello and I tell him why I'm there.

I don't want any trouble, he says.

I can leave your name out if you'd prefer.

That would be good.

The woman is standing next to him.

Go on, tell her, she urges him.

A friend and I used to come here all the time, to the bit just over there. The reservoir would fill up when it rained and there was always fishing. It was so shallow you could do it just with a stick. To hit the fish with, you know? Anyway, that's what we were doing the morning we saw the Quevedo girl under a tree on the shore. We were young. It scared us shitless and we ran to find an adult.

He falls silent and goes on loading the spoon with baby food and seeking out the little girl's mouth. She stares at me with her large eyes.

And tell her the bit your mother always tells, the woman says. She seems to be finding her husband's story incomplete.

They made our lives hell after that, back and forth from court all the time, endless questions. That's why I said I don't want trouble. We had enough of it back then.

When I leave, the woman follows me and pokes her head round the door.

See if you can do something about the flies, she says. We can't even drink *mate* outside, there are so many. Maybe you can report it in the paper, eh?

And she shuts the door quickly so the swarm doesn't slip inside.

I walk slowly towards the wasteland. The weeds would come up to my knees so I stay on the road, out of fear of snakes. There's no sign of the reservoir, that watery bed that cradled María Luisa before she came to rest on the table at the morgue, and then in the municipal cemetery.

I think about the man I've just spoken to. I think about the ironies of fate. The neighbourhood where he lives seems pretty new, it can't be more than ten years old. The houses are allocated by a lottery. That he should end up with one right opposite the place where he saw the most horrific sight of his life: the swollen body of the teenager, her face and one eye eaten by the birds.

Those bones resting in a niche together with the bones of the boy who died young, from a heart attack, and the baby who was just beginning to live, are not the remains of Sarita Mundín. Where are you, Sarita? Who is the other dead girl?

A sign at the entrance to the San José cemetery says it closes at six on Sundays. There are fifteen minutes left. I go in and glance around for the attendant so I can ask where Andrea's grave is. The guy's nowhere to be seen, so I start looking by myself. I decide to begin with the burial niches. I try the ones in the back wall, but the dates are from a long time ago. I move to one of the sides. These are more recent. I scan them quickly, up, down. Nothing. Where's the attendant gone? I'm running out of time. I'm going to have to leave without visiting her.

I hear laughter, muffled by the walls of the tombs. I follow the sound. It's two teenage girls, heading for the exit. They're laughing, who knows what about. I intercept them.

I'm looking for a niche. Maybe you've heard of Andrea Danne, a girl...

Yeah, the one who got killed in her house.

Uh-huh.

I think she's over there, one girl tells me. When I was younger I used to come here all the time, but I haven't been in a while. I think it was over there.

I hurry in the direction they're pointing. I read names, up, down, dates, I look at photos. Until, finally, Andrea. The front of the niche is marble, the colour of milky tea. As well as the plaque with her boyfriend's inscription, there's one from her family and another from her school-mates, the Class of '85. A simple cross, and a photo of her smiling, her long blonde hair loose, wavy and with a few coloured braids. In two vases, purple daisies, orange roses and some stems of white freesias.

They're the same flowers that decorate her father's niche, one row down – no marble front, just bare concrete and the name written in chalk – and her mother's, also unfinished and with a sign attached, made on the computer, giving her name and the date of her death.

I leave at six on the dot. As soon as I'm through the gates I hear a noise behind me. It must be the attendant, I think, but I don't turn round to see.

They say that when you're leaving a cemetery, you should never, ever look back.

EPILOGUE

The new year began a month ago. In that time, at least ten women have been killed for being women. I say at least because these are the names that appeared in the papers, the ones that counted as news.

Mariela Bustos, stabbed twenty-two times, in Las Caleras, Córdoba. Marina Soledad Da Silva, beaten and thrown down a well, in Nemesio Parma, Misiones. Zulma Brochero, knifed in the forehead, and Arnulfa Ríos, shot, both in Río Segundo, Córdoba. Paola Tomé, strangled, in Junín, Buenos Aires. Priscila Lafuente, beaten to death, half-burned on a barbecue and then thrown in a stream, in Berazategui. Carolina Arcos, killed with a blow to the head, on a building site in Rafaela, Santa Fe. Nanci Molina, stabbed, in Presidencia de la Plaza, Chaco. Luciana Rodríguez, beaten to death, in the capital of Mendoza. Querlinda Vásquez, strangled, in Las Heras, Santa Cruz.

We're in summer now and it's hot, almost like the morning of November 16th, 1986, when, in a way, this book began to be written, when the dead girl crossed my path. Now I'm forty and, unlike her and the thousands of women murdered in my country since then, I'm still alive. Purely a matter of luck.

Yesterday I said goodbye to the Señora. The pack of tarot cards was in the green cloth as usual, but we didn't touch them, I didn't move the cards in circles with my right hand, I didn't ask any questions. She told me it's time to let go, that it's not good to spend too long drifting from one side to the other, from life into death. That now the girls have to go back to where they belong.

As she said this, she reached over the table between us and took my hand in hers. Squeezing it, each of us sitting where we'd sat in every session. I squeezed her hand back and then gradually she began to let go. I held on a little, a moment longer, I could still feel the girls through her. She looked at me. Or they looked at me and I understood and I began to let go as well.

Three white candles. My farewell to the girls.

One white candle for Andrea. One white candle for María Luisa. One white candle for Sarita, and if Sarita is alive, please let her be alive, then the candle is for that nameless girl who washed up on the banks of the Tcalamochita river over twenty years ago. The same wish for all of them: sleep well.

I spent the summer before Andrea's murder in the countryside, at my grandparents' place. It was the last summer I'd spend there with my aunt Liliana, who was about to get married and move to the town, to her new house. In the siesta one day we went to see Teya, her neighbour and confidante, a woman with grown-up children. It was about three miles from my grandpa's farm to Teya's. That year I'd had a growth spurt and was as tall as my aunt, who was a short woman. We walked along arm in arm, and slowly, though the sun was fierce. I knew my aunt wouldn't be the same after she got married, that this intimate bond we'd shared ever since I was little, and that had become closer as I grew up, wouldn't be the same either. From then on, she would live with a man, her husband. We'd never again sleep in the same bed, or be able to stay up until all hours chatting about nothing. That walk was special.

I didn't say anything because I didn't want us to get sad. But I think she was feeling something similar. Then she told me a story I'd always heard in bits, the way children eavesdrop on conversations they shouldn't. I don't know if she told me by chance or because she also sensed the finality of that walk through the countryside and wanted to tell me something that was important to her.

A few years back, she'd been walking by herself along that same dirt track. On the way to Teya's again, at siesta time, to listen to the radio under the trees, drink *mate* and gossip. Halfway there, a figure emerged from the crops that grew on each side of the little dirt track: Tatú, a cousin in his forties who'd been ogling her for a long time. Tatú was single and had never been known to have a girlfriend or go to a dance.

What are you doing, you klutz, you scared me, my aunt said, then turned to carry on her way. But he didn't answer and grabbed hold of her arm, so hard it seemed he might yank it from the socket. My aunt tried to struggle free and he seized her other arm. For a moment he was so close she could smell the wine and cigarettes on his breath, his eyes like two burning coals. He began to drag her with him. He wanted to get her into the cornfield.

I thought once he had me in there, first he'd rape me then he'd kill me, she said in a trembling voice. I'm sure he was going to kill me.

Tatú was a strong man, but he was also drunk and heady with lust. My aunt was a slight girl. She could never explain how she found the strength to shake off those calloused hands clutching her arms. But she managed to wriggle free and even give him a shove that sent him staggering back into the dusty rubble in the ditch. She ran and ran until she thought she might burst, like horses do.

I've never been so afraid and I've never been so brave as I was then, she said.

Her eyes were shining, but perhaps it was the sun, so strong the landscape shimmered in the distance.

After that, her grandfather gave Tatú a beating and he never went near my aunt again, or, I hope, any other girl.

We carried on walking, pressed closer together now, our arms sticky from the heat.

The north wind made the rough leaves of the corn rub together and the stems sway from side to side, producing a menacing sound that, if you listened closely, could also be the music of a small victory.

Buenos Aires, 30th January 2014

ACKNOWLEDGEMENTS

To Silvia Promeslavsky, for being my local guide in the *indefinite zone*.

To the relatives and friends of Andrea, María Luisa and Sarita, who provided their testimony for the book.

To the judges Cristina Calaveyra, Oscar Sudría and Mariano Miño, and the public prosecutor Rodolfo Lineras.

To Mary Amaya and Mónica Fornero from the Real Truth, Justice for All association.

To the journalists María Dora Flores, Gustavo Saldaña and Sergio Vaudagnotto.

To Argentina's Fondo Nacional de las Artes.

Director & Editor: Carolina Orloff
Director: Samuel McDowell

www.charcopress.com

Dead Girls was published on
80gsm Munken Premium Cream paper.

The text was designed using
Bembo 11.5 and ITC Galliard.

Printed in March 2024 by TJ Books
Padstow, Cornwall, PL28 8RW using responsibly sourced paper
and environmentally-friendly adhesive.